DELAYED

TJ Lee

TJ Lee

Copyright © 2024 The Weird World of TJ Lee

ISBN: 979-8-9899988-0-7

DEDICATION

To all the dads out there that give their all to take care of their families.

CHAPTER 1

Angie

"You sure I can't convince you to move out west? It's sunny all year round." Whit pleaded with me for the five hundredth time in the last few days. She already knew the answer, and knew it wasn't going to be changing anytime soon, but the woman just had to keep trying her luck.

I gave her an amused smile and shook my head with a sigh. "It's sunny in Florida too."

She pouted, with a slight grimace. "Yeah, but our wind blows straight. None of that circular crap."

I laughed, and then laughed some more. "I'd rather that than the earth randomly moving under my feet."

She clicked her tongue as she turned her head away from me. "You need a little earth moving action."

I gave a soft snort. "Who you tellin?" My younger, more immature side had a habit of coming out when I was with her and our other friends. It happened to all of us. Anytime we got together, it was like we automatically reverted back fifteen years.

Knowing she'd lost the battle, again, Whit gave me a hug. "I'll miss ya. Call me tomorrow. Let me know you're safe."

"What, you don't want me to call tonight?"

Whit blushed slightly. "I got plans tonight."

I bumped her with my elbow and winked. "Got your own earth moving action planned?"

Her blush took flight, and I laughed some more. I was happy for her. She and her husband had been married for nearly ten years, and they were still going strong. Apparently that was physically too.

Whit and I hugged tight one more time as we said goodbye outside her gate. Our annual trips every year were always bitter sweet. We had so much fun together, but saying goodbye was always hard. Every year we chose one place, within the continental United States, and met up at the end of every summer.

Natalie "Nat" Winters, Laura White, Whitney "Whit" Anders, and me (Angela "Angie" Carson) roomed together the last three years of college at Florida State University. Not one of us had been Tallahassee locals, we were all transplants. Nat was from Georgia. Laura was from Louisiana. I was from Miami. And Whit was from California. After my first year in the dorms, I got approved for off campus housing. We all shared an apartment together for the remainder of our time there. Best choice I ever made. For one, I wasn't sharing my bathroom with two dozen other girls. It was a small apartment. 2 bedrooms, 1 bathroom. But it was our haven, our escape from the stress of college life.

Sadly, with all of us being from different states, it made it a bit harder to stay in touch after we graduated. We made a four-way pinky promise that we would all meet up every summer for one weekend, no matter what was going on in our lives. And that was to be kept separate from big events, like weddings and such. It hadn't been easy, but we'd made it work.

Take five years ago for example, when Whit was nine months pregnant with her and her husband's first baby. We made Los Angeles our vacay spot. Allen was great, he gave us our space to keep our tradition going. And we all were able to be there when walking around Santa Monica Pier pushed baby Carolyn out a tad bit early.

This year we chose to go to Las Vegas, celebrating ten years of roomie reunions. Laura and Whit decided to gang up on Nat and me. They had the goal of at least one of us getting drunk married. All because she and I were still single. Leave it to the happily married, twitterpated ones to try to shove that happiness on the rest of us. They had good hearts, but not the best laid plans.

Considering I was not a heavy, or even a light, drinker, Nat got the full brunt of it. She got close. She did wake up next to some guy with no idea who he was. Unfortunately, no ring was on that finger.

Nat and Laura were on the same flight back. Well, the first part anyway. Laura had one more short flight to go after they split. They left first, around two in the afternoon. Which left Whit and me. My flight was last, so I chose to hang out near her gate with her. Get all the time I could with her before she was gone too.

Before it would just be me.

After saying goodbye, I stopped into the closest bathroom to clean myself up. Whit always managed to turn my waterworks on. We all may be close, but when it came down to it, she was my bestie. She was my ride or die. And she had never given up trying to convince me to move out to California.
Not long after Carolyn was born, they moved out of the city. I'd admit, it was tempting at times to take her up on it. Especially after our group vacations. I hated saying goodbye, and she knew that.

Every year, she tried.

Every year, I turned her down.

I had family and good friends in Miami. I had my dad, my cousins, and my kids. Not by birth of course. Or by marriage. They were mine by education. I was a 2nd grade teacher at Morningside Elementary. I'd been there for almost ten years. I loved my school. I loved my home.

I was also a stationary individual. I preferred consistency. I preferred a solid foundation underneath my feet. I had no desire to be moving any time in the near future. Let alone moving across the country.

See, I was a military brat as a kid. My dad was in the Marines for 16 years, 15 of which my mom and I had the privilege of following him around from base to base. We did live in some pretty cool areas. I got to see quite a bit of the world. But it also got really tiring. The worst part was that even though we moved to be with him, dad wasn't really around all that often.

After mom died, dad was granted a hardship discharge, and he moved us home to Miami. It was where he and mom had grown up and the rest of our family still lived.

I had enough of moving. I liked having firm ground under me, preferably one that didn't shake randomly (at least we knew when a hurricane was coming). I learned the joy of stability and never wanted to change that. Going away to college was the only time I had left Miami since we officially moved there when I was a teenager.

 I only left because I had recently broken up with my boyfriend and needed a change of scenery for a while. But even there, I stayed with the same roommates, in the same apartment, for three years.

After a quick clean-up, which wasn't hard, seeing as I rarely wore all that much makeup, I headed over to my terminal. Thankfully I had a direct flight, I had no desire to wait in another airport for hours on end. I found my gate, then strolled to find a place to hang out. My flight was due to leave at six, so I still had another two hours to kill.

I was anxious to get home as the weather app on my phone was warning me that a tropical storm would be hitting Miami tomorrow. Hence Whit trying to use the lovely winds of Miami to convince me to move. The storms never bothered me though. I just wanted to get back so I could prepare my little bungalow for it.

During my exploration of the terminal, I found a quaint little bar and grill two gates down, which was slowly picking up. More people were beginning to congregate between flights or arriving to wait for the first leg of their journeys.

I took a seat up at the bar and ordered myself a Sprite. That was usually enough to help calm my nerves and any butterflies flying around in my stomach. My eyes glanced up to one of the televisions playing, the one with the news. I had no interest in watching the sports playing on the other two screens.

My eyes took a second to focus on the captions of the muted screen, and then my brain a moment longer to catch up to what I was seeing. I nearly choked on my drink. I ended up grabbing a napkin out of the canister on the counter top to wipe the streaks dripping down my chin from my very graceful moment.

Tropical Storm Edith has been upgraded to a category 3 Hurricane. It is expected to hit landfall around nine tonight.

The map showed the ugly red circle moving from the Keys up through Florida's East Coastline.

I mumbled a curse under my breath and quickly pulled out my phone. Thanks to smartphones and internet access, I was able to check the status of my flight without leaving my bar stool. This place was freaking huge, so I was grateful for that convenience. I had no idea where the monitors were that showed departure and arrival times. And really didn't feel like walking all over again to try and find it.

Sure enough, an hour ago my flight had been marked as delayed. When I was knee deep in conversation with Whit, on the other side of the airport. Just my luck.
I might just blame this on Whit. She jinxed me with her comment about the winds.

With a depressed and resigned sigh, I scoped out the seating arrangements in the restaurant. I spotted a small booth toward the back that was still empty, might as well make myself comfortable. I grabbed my drink and moved to sit down. I chose the side with my back to the room. I didn't care to make eye contact with anyone at the moment, then I might feel the need to acknowledge them, so I wouldn't be rude. I was in the mood to wallow and throw a pity party.

As soon as I sat down, I pushed the call button on my phone.

"Hey, buttercup."

I smiled at my dad's greeting. No matter how old I got, I was always going to be his buttercup. "Hey, daddy." Just like he would always be my daddy.

"Uh, oh. You don't sound very happy. Let me guess. You saw the news." He was one of my best friends for a reason.

"Yep."

"Will the hotel put you up for another night?"

I laughed sarcastically. "Daddy. Nat, and Laura's flight was at two. I've been at the airport since noon."

I heard him suck in a breath with a hiss. "Why don't you call and see if you can get a hotel somewhere nearby, then?"

I gave him a defeated sigh, letting him hear how I felt since he couldn't see my facial expressions. "It's fine. So far my flight has only been delayed. Do you have the house boarded up already?" He should, my dad was always quick to do that.

"Yep." He answered proudly. "Just finished up at your place, too." I grinned, feeling a little lighter. "You're the best, dad. Thank you." I got lucky in the dad department. He really was the World's Best Dad. I dared anybody to try and top my old man.

"Ah, don't mention it." I could hear the embarrassment in his voice. He'd never been comfortable getting praise. But he deserved it. "How are your friends? How was your trip?"

"They're good. Laura is pregnant. Again." I laughed, but more at the way he was practically barking on the other end of the phone.

"How many does this make now?"

"Four. Chuck is crossing his fingers for a boy this time."

My dad whistled. "Can't say I blame him. What about Nat? She still dating that doctor?"

My smile slipped. "No. She got tired of coming in second to his ego."

My dad hmphed. "And what about Whit?"

I giggled. I loved that he cared so much about my life and my friends. My whole life he was like that. Even when he was still active in the Marines. Every time he came home, he asked a hundred questions about every aspect of my life. He wanted every detail he missed. And it always made me feel good that he didn't want to miss anything, even though he was away half the time. I never doubted where I stood in his life.

"Whit's good. The miscarriage last year was hard on both her and Allen, but they are doing better. They are talking about trying again soon."

"That's good. It's never easy losing a child, no matter how far along they were." He should know. Mom miscarried twice. Once before me and once after. Dad had been deployed for both, leaving her alone to deal with the emotional whiplash. "Did she convince you to move yet?"

I laughed loudly. Did I sound like him when I laughed? I really hoped not. He sounded like a dog.

"No, but she sure is trying hard. Now that Carolyn is in school, she is trying to convince me to come teach out there. They are loving suburban life though."

We talked for a few more minutes about my friends and what they had going on. My dad was always so easy to talk to. He knew things that even my best friends didn't know. Mostly because he was there for the downfall of it. Someone had to hold me together during what I thought was the end of the world. When the man you loved rip down every promise you ever made to each other- it kind of was. Especially at 17.

"Well, buttercup, let me know when you get clearance to leave, that way I can be there to pick you up. Oh, and I forgot to tell you. I heard from Jace."

I had to think about who that was for a moment. "Your old buddy from the Marines?"

"Yep, that's the one. You probably don't remember him, but he visited a few times when you were a toddler. Anyway, he finally decided to leave the military behind. He's going to be staying with me for a while. Until he figures out how to be a civilian again."

"Awe, that's great. I'm glad you will be there to help him." My dad hadn't had it easy when he was discharged. He didn't get an adjustment period. He went straight from being an infantry Captain to being a single dad of a teenager that had just lost her mom. And he had just lost the love of his life.

I promised to call him later, and to send him regular updates, then hung up. Now I just had to figure out what to do for the next… however long.

CHAPTER 2

Jason

"Are you sure there aren't any other flights going anywhere near Florida, right now?" I pleaded with the ticket agent at the gate. I had no desire to sit in a freaking airport terminal longer than I had too.

"Sorry, sir. All flights in and out of Florida have been delayed because of the weather. If anything opens back up, we will make an announcement."

"Yeah. Got it." I tried to swallow the groan and irritation. I didn't want to be *that* guy. "And the luggage that I checked for this flight?"

"Will be held. If this flight gets canceled, it will be moved to your new flight when we issue your new ticket."

"Right." Because I totally believed my luggage was *not* going to get lost when that happened.
I missed the Marines.

I missed flying no-class in a cargo plane with a hundred other stinky, sweaty, men. The seats sucked. There weren't any real seat belts. No amenities whatsoever to speak of. And you felt every jerk from the turbulence, making it feel like the plane was going to fall apart any minute.

I missed the Marines.

Biting back the urge to yell at someone, since this wasn't anyone but Mother Nature's fault, I pushed away from the gate and went back to the seat I had already been in for the last hour.

Ten minutes later, I got back up and started walking around. This was too much sitting for me. Too much time with nothing to do.

I spent the majority of the last year behind a desk. All because of a sniper who didn't like the fact that my men and I were rebuilding a school in Iraq. The school welcomed anybody that wanted to learn. Boys and girls.

That was what I'd been doing for the better part of the last 20 plus years. Helping rebuild communities in Iraq, Afghanistan, and other places that were hit the hardest from war and terrorism. When I first joined the Marines, it was as an infantryman. It was alright. But when it came time to re-up, I wasn't going to do it. At least, not until they offered me a spot with the combat engineers. When they asked what my other plans were, I told them it was to work construction. They knew they had me then.

I found my passion there. I found a mission, a purpose.

And then it all got shot to hell, literally.

After the bullet was removed from my thigh, the Powers That Be put my butt behind a desk. But that wasn't the kind of officer I wanted to be. Eventually I was given the option, stay in an air-conditioned office, deciding where the company would go next, or retire.

It was a hard choice. The Marines had been my life for so long. Pretty much my entire adult life.

Searching for guidance, I talked to one of my best friends, someone I hadn't seen in over a decade. His response, "retire your old butt and get over here. We've got plenty of people that need homes to live in."

So, I did. I retired my old butt and now here I was, wandering aimlessly through airport stores. Missing the life I left behind. Wondering if I made the biggest mistake of my life.

I spent more of my life in the Marines than out of it. What did I know about living a civilian life? Last time I was a civilian I had been little more than a kid.

I felt the buzz in the back pocket of my jeans. Civvy clothes. Just one of the many things I was going to have to get used too, fewer pockets. I grinned when I saw the name, already feeling better.

"What do you want, old man?"

He laughed. It felt good to hear it again. You can talk to people via letters and emails, but it's not the same as hearing their voice. It wasn't exactly cheap to make calls from the other side of the world. And the signal always sucked if you tried to do skype. I usually let the guys with families of their own use all our time with those. I had no need.

"Old? I ain't old. You're the one who's retired and walking with a limp. You get the package I sent you?"

My laugh came out of nowhere, making the actual older lady next to me jump. Last month, Marcus sent me a walker. Along with a set of tennis balls to put on the legs. The walker was black and red and had a built-in stool so I could sit down when I needed a break.

"I did, yes. My uncle thanks you."

I spent the last couple weeks with my Uncle Roger, who lived up to his namesake - Mr. Rogers. My mother died of an overdose when I was five. I never knew my father. Roger and his wife took me in, raising me with their own kids. Not once did they ever make me feel like I was a burden or not part of the family.

He was the reason I went into Combat Engineering. Roger was a roofer by trade. He took me on job sites as soon as I was old enough to work. If I hadn't re-upped, I would have gone to work with him.

Marcus snorted. "I figured you would give it to him. How is the old coot?"

"He's well. Hit seventy last month. Not impressed that I would rather work with you then him. But he understands why."

Both our tempers sobered quickly with my statement. Transitions weren't easy, everyone knew that. Thankfully, my Uncle was a Vet himself. He knew the importance my old buddy would be to me during this time. He said he'd rather lose me temporarily than permanently.

"How are you doing?"

I cleared my throat and walked out of the small store. I was going to need a drink, a stiff one at that. "I'm okay. Sitting in this airport is making me itchy though."

"Lots of people, lots of unknowns."

I nodded my agreement, even though he couldn't see me.

"Your flight get delayed?"

"Yes, sir. And now I have too much down time."
He hissed. "You going to be alright?"

Downtime wasn't exactly a fun place to be when you weren't used to it. Downtime also gave insurgents a chance to sneak up on you. There was no such thing as downtime in the military.

I shrugged, pausing in the doorway of a bar and grill near my gate. As was my habit, I scanned the room before entering. There were a lot of people there. Hardly any seats left. "Do I have a choice?"

"Of course, you do. You could get a hotel. You could find yourself a bar and get drunk. Or you could find a really pretty woman who is as bored as you are and let off some steam."

I choked on air, not expecting that last one.

"Don't worry, I don't actually expect you to, it's not who you are." His chuckle was a bit sardonic now.

"I didn't think it was who you were either."

Back in the old days, when we went out to bars with our buddies, we usually sat in the back and just talked over a cold beer. It was how we became such good friends. We were both raised on construction sites, and neither of us cared for the club scene. Given, Marcus was married, and he worshipped the ground his wife walked on, but he still didn't agree with the way the others let loose.

Especially the sailors.

"I'm not. But, as Angela likes to remind me, we're both getting older now. It's okay to move on. I did my duty to her." He grumbled incoherently, obviously disagreeing with that.

I chuckled. I hadn't seen Angela since her tenth birthday, but even then, she was a stubborn and mature little girl. She wanted books, not dolls, for her birthdays. And she didn't do Princess parties.

"She's not wrong, you know."

Marcus sighed. "I know. I know. I've gone on a few dates here and there. But it's not the same. I'm not sure I'll ever find someone again. Not like Marta."

I had never experienced that type of love for myself, at least not from a participating standpoint. I saw them together a few times, and I had seen his face when he talked about her. I never understood how he managed being deployed as often as he did. It was also one of the reasons I had a hard time being at their house. It made me want something I wasn't going to have.

I was 45 years old and retired. I dated many women in my time, all over the world. Even had a few I really liked. But that was it. Love just wasn't in the cards for me. Kids, family, none of that was in the cards for me. Not anymore at least. Some things you outgrew without realizing it.

"Look, do yourself a favor, find someone to talk to. That's all I'm saying."

I shook my head and found an empty stool near the bar. I'd walked around enough that my thigh was beginning to pinch. The stool wasn't going to work for long either. As much as I didn't want to go back to the gate and wait, I needed a real seat. And this place was full.

"Ya huh. We'll see." My eyes rose to the television screens mounted on the walls. I cursed under my breath. "Maybe you should worry about yourself. That looks like one hell of a storm coming your way."

Marcus tskd. "Nah. I'm good. I'm a pro at these by now. Besides, it's only a category 3. That's like a walk on the beach kind of weather."

"Ya huh, just be careful."

We signed off and I ordered myself a beer. Normally I wouldn't drink before flying, but I had a feeling it would be long out of my system by the time I actually got to board a plane.

And just like that, I jinxed myself. My luck just kept sliding down hill.

"Your attention please, Las Vegas airport passengers. All flights headed to Florida have been canceled. Again, all flights headed to Florida have been canceled."

My chin dropped to my chest. My groan was drowned out by hundreds around the terminal. Still, one small whimper and head bang reached my ears. I looked up and saw long brown hair banging multiple times against a table in the back.

Chuckling, I couldn't resist. I walked over to the lone passenger and stood next to her. The banging stopped and a pair of light brown eyes met mine. They reminded me of the desert storms we had to hide from many, many times. They were the color of the sand that covered the grounds. The same color as the wood we used to build with. Her hair was just a few shades darker than that.

"Mind if I join you? There aren't that many seats left around here." I asked, giving her a soft smile. Praying like hell she couldn't hear how hard my chest was pounding. I'd never seen anyone as beautiful as her.

"Uh, yeah, sure. Are you stuck here too?" Her voice was as smooth as the sand dunes.

"Yep. What joy is ours?" I asked, as I set my carry on inside the booth and sat down. She smiled, a bit sadly. "You going on vacation or heading home?"

"I'm on my way home *from* vacation actually." Her eyes dropped from mine and focused on the nails she was picking at. "What about you?"

"Not really sure, actually."

Her eyes came up again, the curiosity brimming. "How do you not know?"

"I'm going to Miami for work. Haven't decided if it will be homebase yet or not."

She nodded. "That makes sense. I'm Angie, by the way." She lifted a hand over the table, and I happily met it.
"Jason." I didn't know why I gave her my full name. It just slipped out. I hadn't gone by Jason in years, decades really.

"Nice to meet you, Jason."

"The pleasure is definitely mine, Angie." My grin grew with the blush that crossed her cheeks. It got even darker when she realized I was still holding her hand. Reluctantly, I let it go.

"So, what is it that you do?"

"I'm in construction." The short answer. People always acted interested about the military part, but they understood next to nothing.

Her eyes lit up. "Really? What kind?"

"All kinds. I've spent the last twenty years building houses from scratch."

"My dad's side of the family is mostly construction workers. It's not an easy job. Where were you building before?"

"All over, mostly other countries. My uncle was a roofer and taught me the trade. I joined the military right out of high school." Why was I telling her all of this?

"Did you do combat engineering then? What branch?"

Huh. "Marines."

She nodded. "My dad was a Marine. We moved all over when I was kid." She shrugged. "Guess that's why I refuse to leave Miami. I like being stationary."

I chuckled. "Yeah, that's something I am looking forward to. Setting roots down somewhere."

I waited for her to ask the why I left questions, everyone did. But she didn't.

"I bet. It must be hard. I'm glad you're working though. My dad always said having a purpose after is what helped him. Personally, I couldn't do it. I got enough of all the moves as a kid."

I chuckled at the face she made, like she had a bad taste in her mouth. "What is it that you do, Angie?"

Her smile lit up her face. "I teach second grade. I absolutely love it. The kids aren't too snotty yet, but they are coming into their own personalities. It's fun to help mold them and to help them satisfy their curiosities."

I eagerly leaned forward onto the table; my hands clasped in front of me. "I've only known teachers in other countries. None here. My last post was building schools in Iraq."

Her beautiful eyes widened. "That must have been so hard. When I first started teaching, I wanted to teach in third world countries. My father put his foot down and refused to hear of it. I could have done it anyway, but he was still raw from losing my mom."

I nodded. He was probably like Marcus then. "Can't say I blame him. It's dangerous over there. How long have you been teaching?"

She gave me that smile and look that said she knew what I was really asking. "I've been teaching for about ten years now. Still love it as much as I did on the first day."

Well, at least she wasn't *half* my age. Just about a quarter younger. That wasn't as bad.

"How long were you in the Marines?"

I chuckled softly, turnabout's fair play. "27 years."

She whistled but gave no other reaction. Interesting. "That's a long time. Why did you leave after so long?"

I brought it on myself. I could have kept us completely on her. "Sniper hit, into my thigh. It was either retirement or desk duty."

She smirked at the look I made. I had copied her same look of disgust from earlier..

"What's your favorite subject to teach?"

Her head dipped to her right and her long brown hair, nearly the same shade as her eyes with the light shining through it, dropped to one side. "Hmm. That's a hard question. But maybe Science. We get to have a lot of fun experiments. And the kids are still young enough that it hasn't hit the gross stage yet."

I sat back and laughed, stretching my arm across the back of the booth I was sitting on. Her eyes tracked my movement and subtly checked out my torso. Guess the age difference didn't scare her off then.

"So, no frog dissections for you?"

She grimaced. It was adorable. "Hell, no. Most of our stuff blends in with art."

A waiter came over and we both looked up. Oddly, I had forgotten we were surrounded by so many people. That was a first for me. I wasn't sure how I felt about that.

"Can I get you folks something to eat or anything else from the bar?"
Angie sighed, as though she was giving in and accepting defeat. "Can I get a coke please? And an order of chicken strips with fries? Oh, and two sides of Ranch."

I expected her to shrug or make some excuse for all the fattening food, but she didn't. She didn't even blink an eye.

"And you, sir?" The waiter turned to me.

"Cherry Coke. And one of those bacon burgers with fries, please."

I waited until the waiter left before turning back to her. "What were you doing in Vegas?"

"My annual *Roomies Reunion.*"

I raised an eyebrow at her, not having a clue what that was. She giggled and blushed.

"It's this thing I do every year with my old roommates from college. No matter what is going on in our lives, we meet up in a neutral place for a vacation. Usually toward the end of summer break."

CHAPTER 3

Angie

Why was this god among men sitting here listening to me run my mouth about my college roommates? Surely there were more interesting, and definitely prettier, people around here that he could talk too. At first, I thought he was just that bored, but he seemed genuinely interested in what I was saying.

Why?

I long ago accepted that I was on the plain side of the looks scale. I was average. For work and going out, yeah, I'd do my make up and get dressed up. That helped. But not when traveling.

Why didn't I let Nat do my makeup this morning again? She begged me!

She was raised by a beautician, and it was her favorite hobby, for crying out loud! I used to let her do it all the time in college. She taught me lots of easy tricks.

I tried not to look at the man's eyes directly. I was too nervous. I was afraid he would get tired of looking at Plain Jane sitting across from him.

Like, seriously, there was nothing special about me. I was average weight, on a good day. Average height. My hair and eyes were plain old brown. Put me in front of a brown backdrop and I would disappear.

I was sure even the waiter was wondering what this guy was doing with me. And it wouldn't have had anything to do with our age difference either. At least he was younger than my dad. That was my dad's limitations when I started dating. Older than me, and younger than him.

Jason had to be at least two inches taller than my dad, who only hits six feet when he spikes his hair. Yeah, that wasn't a pretty phase in his transition to being a civilian. Talk about embarrassing your teenage daughter.

Jason had black hair, with the slightest touch of gray starting on the sides. It made him look distinguished. He had dark brown eyes that looked like fudge sauce. I loved fudge sauce.

I finally stopped rambling nervously when the waiter returned with our drinks. Desperate for a way to shut my mouth up, I grabbed the drink he set down in front of me, trying not to look as awkward as I felt, and took a long drink.

Holy smokes, did it taste good, too. I didn't remember a coke ever tasting so sweet. It took me about three seconds, and two long sips, to figure out why. Just long enough for the panic to set in.

I cursed, repeatedly, pushing the cup away.

Jason jumped forward, his hand catching the glass before it fell over from how hard I pushed it. "What? What's wrong?"

I grabbed my purse and dumped it on the table, not caring the least bit about what I looked like anymore, or what fell out of my purse.

"They must have mixed our drinks up." I coughed, then coughed again. Then cursed again when my eyes started to blur.

"Okay, and?" He sounded like he wasn't sure whether he should be freaking out with me. I must not look bad on the outside yet. That was something at least.

"I'm allergic to cherries. Like, bad." I coughed again. "Can't… find…" lovely my tongue was starting to swell in the back.

At least Jason was smart enough to figure out what I was looking for. He reached into the mess I made and came out with my Epi pen. He jumped around the table and jammed that sucker right into my thigh.

Air hit my lungs within seconds, and I blinked until my eyes cleared. I hadn't even realized I was crying until Jason wiped the tears away with his rough and calloused hands. The kinds of hands I had always preferred on a man. Too many men these days tried to keep them soft. I hated it. People should be true to who they were, not try to hide it.

"Are you okay?" The waiter asked from behind Jason, a little shakily.

"Yeah." I croaked. "Can I get some water please?"

Jason stayed by my side, setting the used pen down carefully on the table. His hand was a little shaky. "Are you sure you're alright?"

I cleared my throat and nodded. "Yes. I hadn't gotten far. Thank you for your help. How did you know what to do?"

"I had a buddy in the corps who had a peanut allergy. He couldn't even be in the same room as them."

I forced out a laugh. "That would suck. I love peanut butter." His grin was even more forced. "I'm okay. Really."

Why did I feel the need to comfort someone who was barely more than a stranger? Still. I lifted my hand and placed it on his cheek. I nearly got lost in his eyes before the waiter returned with my water.

"You can take the cokes back, we're gonna stick with water for now." Jason stood up and moved back to his side of the table.

"You don't have to do that." I said softly, the embarrassment finally kicking in. I was really glad my back was to the rest of the room. How many people had just witnessed that?

Jason shook his head and the waiter stepped away with both our cokes. "I'd rather play it safe. It's a good thing you carry that with you." He pointed at the empty pen on the table.

Cringing, I began cleaning up the mess I'd made. Thankfully my roomies and I carefully plan around certain times of the month. I didn't have any of *those* in my purse today.

"I didn't used too. Once my dad was home full-time, he insisted." Of course, my mother had the same allergy and didn't carry the pen. Turned out, she really should have.

"It's a good thing too. Those aren't standard issue in basic first aid kits. And we aren't exactly near a hospital."

I felt the small smile fighting to come out. He still sounded shaken by my little episode. It didn't seem like the PTSD kind of shaken either.

"True. Guess I'll have to say the dreaded words when I get home." He lifted that eyebrow again and my heart fluttered. I rolled my eyes. "Dad, you were right." I grimaced. "He'll never let me live it down."

Jason laughed so deeply I felt it in the pit of my stomach. It made me laugh softly, happily. I wasn't sure if my heart was racing from his laugh, or if it was the after effects of the pen. Technically, I should be seen by my doctor. But I was stuck in an airport. I would just have to call her tomorrow and talk to her.

By the time our food came, my body was starting to settle again. I munched lightly on the fries since the epinephrine had a habit of leaving me nauseous. Last thing I wanted was to puke in front of a really, *really* cute guy. Especially one that had just played the hero card for me.

We talked about random things, and I slowly started moving onto my chicken. I had been tempted to get the burger at first, but now I was glad I hadn't. That would have been too heavy right now.

Jason told me about growing up an hour outside of Vegas, and some of his favorite memories in the military. I told him about living on different bases. There were a few we both found common ground at. I doubted they were at the same time. Nor did I want to bring that up. I mean, I was a little kid, and he was a soldier at the time, just like my dad. Thinking about that made it a little weird. Not weird enough to stop talking to him, just weird enough to skip to a new topic.

I excused myself to use the bathroom after I finished eating. I was pleased to see that my face did look completely normal. I put cool water on my face and neck, trying to clean off the dried sweat I could feel all over me. Had I been the kind of girl to carry make-up in my purse, I might have been tempted to add some. But that would have been obvious. Even if Jason was only interested in someone to talk to, it was helping time pass faster. I already made a fool out of myself once, no need to do so again. I was not going to see things that weren't there… like him having interest in a more than just friends type of way.

I had banged my head on the table when I heard the announcement about our flights being canceled because I could have gotten an earlier flight, when I first bought my tickets, but I liked waiting around with my friends. I didn't like the idea of them waiting alone in the airport. So, I always took a later flight.

The real kicker was that I had to be to work early on Monday morning. Staff meetings would take up a day or two, then setting up my classroom, and I would need to start lesson planning. I was hoping for at least one day to adjust to being home, get some laundry done, shopping, etc. Now it looked like I was going to have to add yard cleanup. My neighbors weren't the best at keeping their trees cut and trimmed. The hurricanes usually did it for them. Of course, the hurricanes also usually used my yard as the dumping ground for said tree trimmings.

By the time I got back to the table, it was cleaned up and Jason was leaning against it. I did my own version of lifting an eyebrow, he obviously thought my attempt was amusing.

"Thought maybe we could walk around a little bit, find something to do besides sit here." He looked sheepish and nervous. It was adorable.

When had anybody ever been too nervous to talk to me? Especially someone that looked like him.

Jason lifted a hand in my direction, a silent invitation. With a shy smile of my own, I slipped my hand into his. He lifted his backpack onto his other shoulder and picked up my duffle bag. As he pulled me past our table, I noticed the two twenties sitting on top of the bill. In my head I was squealing. He had been standing directly in front of it, so I couldn't see it before. He was trying to be sneaky about paying for me.

It was sexy as hell.

We walked through one of the many souvenir shops, laughing at some of the ridiculous items they sold there, and the even more ridiculous prices. We tried out the different colognes and perfumes. On the cards, not on us.

We left there and came to a stop at one of the many small groups of slot machines.

"Only in Vegas." He said, shaking his head.

I giggled and pulled him over to one. "Come on. Try your luck."

He took his hand from mine and slid it around my waist, pulling me against his side. "My arms are full, looks like you'll have to play for me."

I laughed and shook my head at him. I started to pull money out of my wallet, but he lifted his hand enough to stop me.

"Back right pocket." He lifted his eyebrows a few times, making me blush.

Not one to back down from a challenge, I turned and stood right in front of him. His dark eyes darkened a shade more, his grip on me tightened. And I was fairly certain something else was growing against my stomach.

Definitely not just after a friendly conversation then.

Feeling possessed, I put my right hand on his back, pushing us closer together. Keeping eye contact with him, I slid my hand down until it was inside his pocket. I waited until his head was lowering closer to mine, then swiftly grabbed his wallet and spun back around. I could hear him laughing and sucking on his top teeth behind me, mumbling.

"Alright, I see how it is."

I sat down on the stool, as he set our bags down next to us, but stayed behind me.

"Okay. What do I do now?" I asked him.

He leaned down into my ear, his hands on my shoulders, and spoke incredibly soft. "You just spent the last four days in Las Vegas, and you don't know how to play a slot machine?"

I closed my eyes and tried not to hum at the feel of his breath on my neck. Pretty sure I failed. Judging by the amused shaking chest behind me anyway.

"Nope. Whit's husband forbade her from gambling. She can be a little… competitive." That was putting it mildly. "We avoided the casinos and stuck to shows and other stuff."

He reached around me, sliding his hand against my side, and pulled a five-dollar bill out of his wallet.

"First, you put the money into the machine." He continued to speak softly and slowly as he lifted the bill up to the money slot. "Then you pull the lever down."

He took my hand again, this time from the back, and placed it on the lever. Keeping his grip over mine, he pulled it back. His hand slowly moved up my arm, stopping at my shoulder.

Who would have thought slot machines could be seductive? Certainly not me.

I focused on the fruit and other symbols spinning in circles, trying to catch my breath. Which wasn't easy with Zeus standing behind me, gently rubbing my shoulders.

I frowned when the three wheels stopped. "You lost." I turned enough to look up at him. "Guess you aren't having any luck today." I teased.

He squeezed my shoulders. "Depends on what we're referring to."

I blushed and turned back. I pulled another bill out and stuck it in the machine. This time we broke even. We played a few more rounds, taking turns pulling the lever. Although he did insist I help him with his turns, calling me his good luck charm. I just snorted and shook my head. He lost every time.

"I don't think I'm your good luck charm." I told him. "More like bad luck. You lose every round." Not that I was doing much better, but at least it wasn't a complete loss.

I stood up and turned to face him, he slid his hand behind my back again. "I beg to differ. My luck has definitely been looking up since I met you."

I blushed, again, feeling a little stupid for the fact that I kept blushing. I wasn't exactly an innocent little princess. Yet, I kept acting like one.

"Maybe I'm just not pushing my luck properly."

I tilted my head to the side, completely lost on what he meant. Instead of explaining further, he just winked and stuck another bill in. He lifted our hands together, then pulled on the lever. Only this time, our hands weren't the only things connected. He lowered his head the same time he lowered our arms. His lips met mine softly. As soon as he released the lever, his hand went behind my head. It wasn't long before the kiss deepened into something more. Something I had never felt before.

Dings erupted next to us and people started shouting. I barely heard any of it. Too soon, he pulled away, but dropped his head against mine.

"See, my good luck charm."

I gave one short, breathless, laugh. Slowly, awareness started coming back to me. A few people were standing around us, patting our backs. I looked over at the slot machine, lit up in lights, and squealed with delight. Jason laughed.

I jumped up and wrapped my arms around his neck. "You won the Jackpot!"

"Certainly, feels like it." He mumbled into my shoulder, holding me tight.

I felt giddy, knowing he wasn't talking about the money.

Our moment was interrupted when an airport employee in a suit walked over and congratulated Jason. He had just won 25,000 dollars. I had never seen anyone win so much before. They insisted on a picture, which he made me stand next to him for.

Once the craziness died down, we did our own celebration by finding a small cafe that had dessert. Jason ordered us one large banana split. He even told them no cherries.

He carried the large bowl to a table, and we sat down. Not across from each other this time either. We sat on the same side.

I immediately dipped my spoon into a mountain of strawberry ice cream covered in fudge sauce, and enjoyed the party that my tastebuds were having.

"What?" I asked, noticing his eyes were on me.

"You have a bit of fudge sauce, right, here." He pointed to the corner of my lip. I moved to get my napkin, but he leaned down instead. "I got it."

My eyes closed again, and the lightest of moans came out, as he slowly licked it off. Then his lips met mine again. After he thoroughly made sure the mess was gone, he sat back with a triumphant grin.

"Perfect."

"Ya huh. Very smooth."

"What? You think I did that just so I could kiss you again?"

"Maybe." I was challenging him, and I didn't care.

He leaned over again, meeting me in the middle. Our lips only met briefly, but it was enough to engrave them to my heart. "I don't need a reason beyond just wanting to kiss you."

I gripped his shirt and pulled him back down. Our ice cream was threatening to melt by the time I released him again.
"Let's play 20 questions." Jason said, the ice cream mid-way to his mouth.

"Seriously?" I crinkled my nose, not sure I wanted to go there, but then again, why not?

"Yeah. What else have we got to do?" He slid the bite of banana and vanilla ice cream in his mouth, then slowly pulled the spoon out. "I'll even be a gentleman and let you go first.

"Alright, fine. First question. How old were you when you lost your virginity? To whom? And where were you?" Jason's jaw dropped in shock, and I laughed. "Come on. This was your idea."

He swallowed and looked like he was sweating bullets. "True. I just figured we would start out slower, with more mundane questions."

I waved it off before sticking my spoon back into the quickly disappearing dessert. "That's no fun."

He made a dramatic show of rolling his eyes. "Fine. Even though that was technically three questions." He raised up three fingers and I blushed. "First, I was 16. I spent the summer working with my uncle helping someone rebuild their barn and update the roof on their house. The farmer's daughter brought me lunch every day. It was our last day there. We, uh, broke in the new barn for them."

I leaned on the table, laughing. "So, your first time was basically a country song?"

His eyes lit up in amusement. "I guess so."

"Was there at least hay in there yet?"

He rubbed his face, trying to hide the blush covering his cheeks. I never thought a man blushing would be so sexy, but it was. "Yes. Now, your turn. Same questions."

Well, that sobered me up. "Nope, that's copying. You have to make up your own."

He chuckled as he shook his head. "That was not the agreement."

"We didn't agree to anything before starting."

"Exactly. No rules. So, answer. It's only fair." He slid his spoon into the last bits of the chocolate ice cream and held it up for me. I leaned in and slowly pulled it off his spoon. His gulp was more satisfying than the ice cream was.

I sighed like this was such a grievous thing to ask. "Fine. I was 16 as well. My high school boyfriend." I shoved the next bite in quickly, not wanting to answer the rest. He was too stubborn though.

"And…." He drew out the word. I cringed. "Come on, I basically admitted to living a country song. How bad can yours be?"

"Fitting room in a sporting goods store."

Pretty sure I broke him with that one. He blinked rapidly like he had just received a major shock.

"Not what you were expecting?" That actually made me a little proud.

"No. Not at all. You don't strike me as the type to go public."

I gave him a one shoulder shrug. "He worked a lot after school and on the weekends. I surprised him on his lunch break. We used to make out in there all the time, and well, you know how those things go." Jason was silent a little longer than I liked, which had me worried I may have scared him off. "What? What are you thinking about so hard over there?"

He made a show of looking through the large windows and down the walkway of the terminal. "I'm wondering if they have any family bathrooms on this level."
I kicked him under the table. He rubbed his leg and laughed.

We spent the next fifteen minutes sharing the ice cream and feeding each other. Our questions were sometimes mundane, as he said, others, not so much.

As we left the cafe, hand in hand again, he asked, "Do you want to keep walking or find somewhere to sit and watch a movie?"

"Sit, I think. How would we watch a movie though?" It would be awkward watching a movie together on one of our phones.

"I have my laptop. We can sit on the floor and set it up with a hotspot." He shrugged, trying to play it off like it wasn't that big of a deal. Even after all the times he kissed me tonight, he still seemed nervous. It was kind of cute.

We found an empty corner, not too far from my gate, which turned out to be *our* gate. He put our bags down and set the computer up, pulling up his Netflix account.

"Why don't you pick something, and I will be right back."

I nodded, he kissed me swiftly, then took off. I chose a movie but paused it until he came back. I checked the news on my phone while I waited. It was nearing ten where we were now. The hurricane had made landfall around eight Florida time. So, recently. I thought about messaging my dad but didn't want to risk waking him. That man could sleep through anything.

I looked up when I saw feet coming my way. Then I laughed. Jason was carrying a blanket over one arm. He dropped down next to me, kissed me again, and then spread the blanket out over our legs.

I put my phone away again and snuggled into his side. I could definitely get used to this.

CHAPTER 4

Jason

I was only planning a quick trip to the bathroom, but I saw a stack of blankets through one of the shop windows and acted on instinct. It was too hot outside for me to have been carrying a jacket on the flight, otherwise I would have given it to Angie to use.

I'd never been so comfortable with someone as I was with her. I could care less about the money I won. Kissing her like that, her kissing me back like she did, I already felt like the richest man alive. No one had ever looked at me the way she did. No one had ever captured my attention the way she did.

When would it be appropriate for me to ask her out? We're both going to be living in Miami. Surely we could find a way to continue what we had started.

The only thing that was holding me back was wondering if this was an airport fling for her, or if she really was in this as much as I was. I didn't get that feeling from her though. She had a down-to-earth sort of personality. But…

Halfway through the movie, I felt her head bob on my shoulder. I looked down and saw Angie's eyes closed. Very carefully, I lowered her to lay down on her duffle bag. Thankfully it was next to her. I pushed it away from the wall enough to put my bag next to hers. Once I had her situated, I slid the computer down, so I could keep her in my arms a little longer.

I was finishing my second movie when the announcement that flights would be resuming in the next few hours came through. Angie didn't budge. Lines were already beginning to form to reserve a post on the first flights out. Very slowly, I pulled my arm out from under her, and moved away. She frowned slightly, once again making me feel like the richest man alive.

I opened her purse and pulled out her boarding pass and ID, then took it with mine over to the ticket counter. I waited in line for nearly an hour, keeping my eyes on Angie. I didn't move them off her until it was my turn.

"Hello." I greeted the overly tired ticket agent.

"Good morning, can I see your boarding pass please?"

"Here, and the other is for my girlfriend who is out cold next to the wall." I pointed at her. The agent barely looked at her before turning back to the computer.

"Okay. I only have one first class seat available on the flight leaving at seven. The next flight won't be until ten, where I can get both of you on."

I swore and looked back at the sleeping angel. I was torn. I wanted to keep her with me. The longer the better, and the more time I would have to try and ask her out. At least get her number. But she was stressing to me earlier about all the things she had to do before the school year started for her. I knew it was only a few hours difference, which really didn't matter in the long run. But it would matter to her.

"Put her in the first-class seat on the earlier flight. I will take the later one."

"Okay. That will be 350 for the upgrade."

I pulled my wallet out again and handed her my card. Even without the winnings, this wouldn't have hurt. 27 years in the military, most of which was spent living in the barracks or a tent. I never had a need for one of the houses on base. It was just me. That being said, I saved a lot of money on housing expenses. Nor had I needed a car of my own.

I waited for our new boarding passes, and the assurances that my luggage would be transferred without any issue. Still crossed my fingers on that one. At least Angie hadn't checked any baggage. That would make her travels a little easier.

I walked back over to her and carefully slid the new boarding pass into her purse. I closed up my computer and put it in the laptop spot inside my bag. Then I laid behind Angie and carefully started pushing my arm under her again. She rolled over and snuggled into my chest before I could finish the move. I wrapped my arm around her, holding her close. With the other, I pulled out my phone and set an alarm. Two hours would be more than enough sleep for me.

I put my phone back in my pocket and pulled the small blanket over her again. I fell asleep faster than I normally would have and had no dreams whatsoever. Another rarity.

I woke up to the sound of my alarm beeping, and the feeling of someone reaching into my pocket and pulling out my phone. I opened my eyes and watched as she turned it off and then slid it back into my pocket.

"You're going to need to charge that phone soon." Angie smiled. "Thank you for laying me down."

I pulled her in and kissed the top of her head. "My pleasure."

She hummed and wrapped her arm around my waist. I gave a contented sigh. That contentment evaporated rather quickly though.

"We should feed you breakfast. Your flight leaves in two hours." She leaned back again, looking up at me. "They made the announcement last night. I was able to get you on the first flight out, at seven."

Someone so beautiful should never look so sad. "What about you?"

"I tried. But there were a lot of people that beat me to the line. There was only one seat left. I won't fly out until later. I almost put you on mine, but I know you have a lot you need to do today."

I expected her to be mad at me, or more offended that I didn't try to put her on my flight. That was not what I got though. What I got was a kiss.

"Thank you. While I wouldn't have complained about being with you, I do need to get back."

I kissed her again. Keeping myself from begging for her number and that date. Her comment could be taken in a few different ways.

I pulled her up, and we gathered our things. We stepped into a Burger King, as not many places were open yet. We each got one of their breakfast sandwiches. I loved that she didn't care about what she ate, as long as it tasted good.

And had no cherries.

I felt more fear during those few small moments than I had when I got shot and fell off the roof I was working on. We had a lot of tools on that ground, and there were more than a few poles sticking out of the foundation as well. Thankfully, I fell toward the back of the house, the debris I hit only left bruises. But that was nothing compared to the fear when I realized Angie was having an extreme allergic reaction to that drink.

After we ate, both of us quieter than we had been the night before, we walked over to her new gate.

I decided I really needed to grow a pair and just ask her. "Can I have your number?"

She threw her head back and laughed. As soon as it came back down I kissed the smile off her face. Well, I kissed the smile anyway. It was still there, after.

"I was wondering if you were going to ask."

I dropped both our bags, and the blanket, and held her against my chest. "You could have always asked."

That blush appeared again. "Technically, yes. But I wasn't sure if you wanted to see me again."

"Why wouldn't I?"

She shrugged, her eyes down. Seems I wasn't the only one who was self-conscious about all of this. It certainly explained a lot. I pinched her chin between my thumb and forefinger, pushing it up until her eyes met mine again.

"I have thoroughly enjoyed spending this time with you, Angie. You are, without a doubt, the most beautiful thing I have ever seen." She blushed and tried to lower her head again. I didn't let her. "This has been more than just a way to kill time for me. I would have asked sooner, but I wasn't sure where you stood."

Once again, instead of speaking, she just kissed me. Which I was good with. It was answer enough. Especially when it was followed up with her phone number. We waited until the plane started boarding, just holding each other.

"I will call you tonight, once I get settled." I promised. I handed her the blanket. "Keep it. Please."

She giggled, then kissed me again. "I'll still be in the air when you take off. So, you better call me tonight. I want to hear all the things you did while waiting." She winked at me and joined her line to board.

I waited near the window, sent her a few messages, and then watched as her plane took off. An ominous feeling sat in my stomach. A feeling I knew was my gut, warning me that things were not going to go as planned. That worried me a bit. Angie had given me hope that maybe I wasn't too old for love after all. She gave me hope that this civilian thing wouldn't be so bad. Not if she was by my side. I wasn't exactly whole, but maybe she could help me get there.

For her, I would make sure that I got there. She gave me a reason to try harder to heal, to create a life.

Hell, to stay in Miami.

I didn't bother looking around the airport again. I'd seen it all many times already. Instead, I sat down and plugged in my phone, as she suggested. I messaged Marcus, while my computer booted up again.

Me: Flight leaves at ten. Did you survive?
Cap: Ha! Takes more than a little wind to send me to Kansas.
Cap: Plenty of damage around here, we're going to be busy the next few weeks.
Me: Good.
Cap: What did you do all night?
Me: Made a new friend. I'll tell you all about her when I get there.
Cap: *emoji with heart eyes*
Me: Shut up.
Cap: Lol. You sure you don't want me to pick you up?
Me: Nah. I don't trust your eyesight.
Cap: *middle finger emoji*

Me: What's with you and all the emojis? You trying to pretend to be young again?
Cap: *shoulder shrug emoji* raised a teenage daughter.

I laughed. Yeah, I guess that would do it. I did the math in my head, trying to figure out how old his daughter would be now. She had to be getting close to thirty. I shivered, a little weirded out by the fact that I was hoping to date a woman around her age. It was a good thing Angie didn't so much as blink an eye when I told her how long I was in the Marines for.

I watched another movie, my mind not focusing on it in the slightest. Instead, it was back on last night. Back on Angie. I would call her as soon as I got settled into Marcus' house. I needed to get myself a car within the next few days and start looking for places. I was too old to be couch surfing. And she deserved a man who was settled.

CHAPTER 5

Angie

I would not cry. I would not cry. I would not cry. I literally met the man twelve hours ago. I was not going to cry.

At least not until tonight. And only if he didn't call. But he was going to call. He promised he would. He seemed like the type to keep his promises.

I think.

"Boarding pass." The haggard looking man at the gate practically demanded. I obediently handed it to him. He punched it and handed it back with a tired smile. "Enjoy your flight."

"Thank you." I held it in my hand and walked down the gangplank.

I felt eyes on me, so I turned in the doorway and waved to Jason. I was not going to cry. I chanted the phrase to myself again as I walked further away from him.

"Pass please." A flight attendant held her hand up for it. I handed the same boarding pass over to her and she looked at it briefly. "Your seat is next to the window, third row on your left."

I looked over to where she pointed, then looked back. "That's first class. I paid for coach." I told her carefully, not wanting it to sound like I was calling her stupid or anything.

She smiled softly. "Someone must have bumped you up." She pointed to the number three on my pass. "Row 3. First class, darling." She waved me forward again, her hand already reaching for the next person's pass.

I stowed my bag up top, and the person sitting in the aisle seat stood up so I could get in. I thanked the older gentleman and sat down in a much wider seat than I was used to.

How did I get first class?

Dumbfounded, I spread the blanket over me and relaxed into the seat. I looked down at the blanket, a smile slowly creeping across my face as realization came to me. Jason. When he traded in my boarding pass, he must have upgraded me. I could kiss him. And I would… when I saw him again.

I pulled my phone out of my purse, then stowed the purse under the seat in front of me.

Me: morning, daddy. I just boarded.
Dad: *confetti emoji*

I laughed and shook my head. He liked to blame me for his emoji use, but he was such a liar.

Dad: I'll be there with bells on to pick you up, buttercup!
Me: What's the damage?
Dad: Nothing but yard clean up over here. Headed to your place now.
Me: Thank you. Gotta go. Love you!

Dad: Love you, too. Can't wait to see you. *kissing heart emoji*

I was still laughing when a new message popped up.

Unknown: I'm already bored.

I quickly saved the number, my grin turning giddy.

Me: You'll survive.
Jason: IDK about that.

What was it with older men and text lingo and emojis?

Jason: Fly safe. I'll talk to you tonight.

My heart warmed. The next message that came through was a picture. The one that had been taken when they gave him his winnings. We stood side by side, but instead of looking at the camera, we were looking at each other. I had a hard time taking my eyes off the man during the whole winning hassle. I was sure he would disappear, and it would all have been the daydream of a bored and lonely woman.

The flight attendants started walking down the aisles, closing the overhead bins. Sniffling, I switched my phone to airplane mode. While buckling, I noticed charging ports in the arm rest.

Hell, yeah.

I pulled my charging cable out of my purse and plugged in my phone and read an eBook for the duration of the flight.

As soon as we started landing procedures, I switched my phone off airplane mode. I was hoping to have a missed message from Jason, but I didn't. It was a ridiculous hope, he was flying right now, and he knew my phone was off before that. I just needed to be patient.

I pulled my things out of the overhead bin and joined the line to disembark from the plane. I didn't need the signs to lead me to baggage claim and the exit, I knew my way around this airport as well as I knew my way home.

It didn't matter that it had only been a few days since I had last seen him, I was always excited to see my dad. I dropped my bag and jumped on him. He laughed. After spending half my life only seeing him on and off for months at a time, it was always good to see each other again. I didn't care if my squeal sounded like a little girl. I loved my dad.

"Hey, buttercup. How was your flight?"

"Awesome. I got bumped up to first class!" I told him happily, as he picked up my bag.

"Nice. How'd that happen?"

"I met a friend last night. We hung out, killing time. I was sleeping when they announced flights resuming soon, so he exchanged my boarding pass for me. And, I believe, upgraded me. He didn't say anything of course. I found out *after* I got on the plane."

The humid August air hit us as we stepped outside. The air always felt fresher to me after a storm blew through. I absolutely loved it. I took a deep breath, enjoying how clean it felt.

"A *he*, huh?" My dad's twinkling eyes met mine.

I laughed and pushed his shoulder, which made him laugh harder. "Yes. A *he*." I rolled my eyes and followed him to the crosswalk. "And that is all I am telling you for now."

We stopped at the crosswalk and waited our turn to get to the parking garage. "Hmm, sounds to me like you like this one."

I couldn't help the blush and accompanying grin. "I do. Now I just have to hope he isn't full of it and calls me tonight when he gets in."

"He didn't fly with you?" And there was the concerned father. "No. There was only one seat left, on this one. He knew I had things to do before work tomorrow. So, he gave it to me and took the later flight."

"That was nice of him. What does he do?"

"Nope, I told you. I'm not telling you a thing." I sighed, my heart slowing as we crossed the street. "I'd like to see him actually call before I get my hopes up."

He must have heard something in my tone. My dad waited until we were alone in the elevator, going up to the third floor before turning to me. "You are just like your mother. You never see yourself the way others do."

"I see myself fine, daddy."

He scoffed and shook his head. I followed him to his pick-up truck. It was still dry and didn't have a scratch on it. Meaning he actually parked it in the garage for a change.

"So, how's my little bungalow?" I asked carefully. He cleared his throat and adjusted his seating. I groaned. "How bad is it?"

"Not too bad. Nothing we can't have fixed within a few days."

"Days? Daddy, I have to work!" I practically screamed in frustration.

"I know, buttercup. Don't worry. With Jace's help, we should have it done in no time. It's just a matter of having the supplies. There are many others with even worse damage."

I grimaced. "Where and what?"

"Your living room. The roof. We could have it done even faster if you want to put in a sunroof there." He curled the corner of his lip into a smile.

"Seriously?"

He chuckled and reached his hand over to pat my knee. "It's not that bad, Ang."

It was. It really was. The neighbor on my right, who didn't know how to trim a freaking tree, lost one completely. It was now taking up residence inside my living room. It fell right through the roof of my cute little three-bedroom bungalow. The place had been falling apart when I bought it, so I got a good price. Dad, grandpa, a few cousins, a couple friends, and I all worked on it for weeks over the summer break.

I stood in my front lawn, still somewhat in the truck, bawling. Dad walked over and put his arm around my shoulders.

"It'll be fine."

"I can't live in it like this. What if it rains?" It always rained. Hence the humidity. "What if another storm blows through soon? They call it hurricane *season* for a reason!"

He ignored my borderline tantrum, knowing it all stemmed from stress and lack of decent sleep. "That's an easy fix. You are going to come stay with me while we fix it up. Your cousins should be here soon to help move the tree and tarp up the roof. In the meantime, you and I can start moving what we can out of the living room."

I nodded, tears sliding down my face, as he pulled me toward the house. Once inside, I detoured to my bedroom, changing into fewer clothes. Heavy lifting and humidity, mixed with jean pants and a baggy shirt, no thank you. I breathed a sigh of relief when I slid on my tank top and jean shorts. Much better.

We spent the next hour moving anything we could out of that room. We had to be careful though, in case the tree sank further in. My cousins showed up soon after with pizza boxes, hugs, and reassurances.

I sat and ate in my bedroom, while they removed the giant tree from my roof. I robotically moved around my room, packing up fresh clothes to take over to my dad's with me. I grabbed my computer, my planners (that I bought new every summer), and all my writing utensils. Looked like I was going to have to prep for this school year from my dad's house.

It took them an hour to get the bulk of the tree off my house. Then another half hour to lay the tarp. We left the portion of the tree that invaded my home, sitting on my lawn. They promised to come over the next day and cut it up into firewood for me. I took a sick amount of satisfaction knowing that sucker was going to pay for destroying my house. I could already picture myself yelling "burn, sucker, burn," every time I threw a log into the fire this winter.

"Hey, buttercup?" My dad hollered as he walked down my hall to me. "I need to head home. Jace's flight just landed. He should be headed toward the house soon. I want to fire up the grill."

I mouthed a curse while my back was still to him, before turning to face him. "Dad, are you sure it's okay if I stay with you? You already have Jace coming."

He just laughed and hugged me, then kissed my forehead. "I have plenty of room. Besides, it'll be nice to have a full house again. Come on over as soon as you are ready."

His eye quirked up in a similar way that Jason's did. His flight should be landing about now too. I hoped that meant I would hear from him soon. I really wished I could just curl up in his arms and cry about my house.

"Fine, if you're sure." I sighed and looked back to my home, knowing I didn't have much of a choice. "I'll only be a few minutes behind you. I just need to grab a few more things." Part of me wanted to do something to my neighbor's perfect house, which had come through the storm without a scratch. But that just wasn't who I was. Even if they did deserve it.

"Alright, see you over there." He kissed the side of my head. "Drive safe. The roads aren't completely cleared yet."

"I know. Thank you."

I said goodbye to my cousins as they left right behind him, then sat in my house, staring at everything out of place. I had books that were damaged from the rain. But those could be replaced. I did get lucky that the television was mounted on the other side of the room. Knowing my luck, that would have started a fire.

With a deep sigh, I forced myself to load up my car. I took out all the perishable food from my fridge and tossed it. I had no power in my house, and who knew what time that went out last night. I loaded all the things from the freezer up. They were still at least half frozen, so I decided to take them to my dad's house with me.

Nearly an hour after he left, so did I.

The streets were mostly clear. There was some debris on the roads, but not too much. A few street lights had fallen to the ground. The further inland I got, toward my dad's house, the less damage there was. That was normal though. I lived closer to the beach, so I usually got hit harder.

I pulled into the driveway, noticing the new car parked on the street. I parked next to my dad's car and grabbed my purse full of notebooks and my planner. He and his little friend could help me with the rest. I let myself in, dropped my purse on the couch, and my keys on a small end table next to the front door. I followed the sounds of talking and laughter floating in from the back porch thanks to the sliding glass door being left open.

My dad sounded happy. Which made me happy.

As I got closer to the screen door, the sound from a deep laugh shot through me. And I froze.

Oh, please, no. No, no, no.

Hadn't I had enough bad luck today?

CHAPTER 6

Jason

I was tempted to message Angie as soon as my plane landed, but I held off. She was probably busy cleaning up and getting ready for the week ahead. I was 45, not 15. It was okay to be eager, but not overly so. I could, and would, be a grownup about this. And not act like a horny teenager.

Even if being around her made me feel younger than I had in years.

Acting like an adult, I messaged Marcus, letting him know that I was there and headed his way. Instead of the emoji, I got one of those GIF things. It was some party one. The man clearly had too much time on his hands. The GIF had a grill going, so I took that to mean that he was grilling. He had always loved to grill, any chance he got. It was comforting to know that he was still the same person he had been when we served together.

Originally, I had planned on taking an Uber from the airport. I wasn't sure if they would be out right now, because of the storm that just passed, and I was hoping to see Angie soon, so I rented a car instead. No doubt, Marcus would have happily let me borrow his truck, but I had too much pride for that. It was bad enough I was going to be living in his house and working for him.

That need to be a grownup was kicking in.

I put his address into the car's GPS and followed it to his place. It was a good thing I was used to driving on roads that had been bombed out. At least these were a few steps up from that. I parked on the street, honking my horn. Marcus came out a minute later, a grin on his face.

"Well, well, well. Look what the hurricane allowed in."

I laughed and met him on the pathway. I hugged him tight and patted his back. He hit my back twice as hard.

"Nice to see you, Cap." He was only a Sergeant when I was in his unit, but when he got promoted, I teased him. It stuck.

He patted my face as we stepped back. "Look at you, all grown up. And a *Major* at that."

I laughed and shook my head. "Are you ever going to let that go?"

"Nope. You want some help? I bet that leg of yours is smartin a bit about now."

It was, in a bad way, but I wasn't going to own up to it. "Nah, it's fine." I popped the trunk, and he helped pull out the few bags I had. I had been relieved to see that the airline had not lost any of my luggage.

"Yah huh. Still full of it, I see." He smirked, leading me into his house. "You know you don't have to do that with me, right? It's kind of the point of you being here."

I gave a frustrated sigh. "Fine. It hurts like hell. I slept on the floor of an airport, then sat on a plane for a few hours. It just needs movement, that's all."

I hissed as I followed him up a flight of stairs. He laughed. "You did say you needed movement."

"Shut up." I croaked, reaching the landing. Thankfully, he had me in the first room on the left.

"Next room over is Angela's. Mine's at the end."

"I thought your girl moved out. I seem to remember getting dozens of letters from someone being all mopey about their baby being all grown up now."

He shrugged. "She is. But her place didn't fare as well as mine did last night. Her neighbor's tree fell on top of her roof. Smashed right through the living room. She should be here soon. I told her she was coming to stay here until we can get it fixed."

"Guess my timing is good then." I grinned at him. "You suck with roofs."

He gave me a fake snarl. "I do not."

He totally did. And he knew it.

Marcus gave up the act quickly. "Come on, I've got the grill heating up in the back. We can grab you an ice pack for that leg on the way. Bathroom is across the hall." He pointed at it as I pulled the bedroom door closed behind me. "You'll have to share with Ang."

"That's fine. Beats sharing it with a dozen men."

He guffawed and nearly lost his step. "That's true. Ang is really easy to live with. She'll probably spend most of the time in her room lesson planning. When she's home that is."

It was my turn to falter in my step. "Angela is a teacher?"

"Yep. Second grade. I was proud as punch when she got her teaching license. She's been in the same school ever since."

"That's good. Stable." I swallowed and stopped at the bottom of the stairs next to him. "Was she home when the roof caved in? Would have given her quite the fright."

Marcus put his arm around my neck and pulled me through to the kitchen. "Nah. She was stuck in the Vegas airport. Come to think of it, I should have had you look for her. I picked her up earlier. She said she met a new friend there, some guy. But won't tell me anymore than that."

I took the ice pack from him in a bit of a daze and followed him onto the porch. The world couldn't be that small. Could it?

It couldn't be that *mean...* could it?

I struggled to think of a question I could ask that wouldn't sound like I was interrogating him about his daughter, he beat me to it though. He jumped right into old stories. I started to relax, laughing along with him. Praying that it was all a coincidence.

Marcus had the same shade of hair color as Angie. A little taller. His eyes were hazel. But there was a small resemblance in the facial structure. And she did say her dad had been in the Marines when she was a kid. Not to mention, she and I both lived on some of the same bases. Neither of us had wanted to delve into whether it was at the same time.

He handed me a beer, which I needed more than he knew. I had my leg propped up on a small table that sat in the middle of a ring of cushioned patio furniture.

"Hey, dad." A slightly wary but familiar voice came from the doorway, her eyes trained on me.

Yep, I was screwed.

Even still, I couldn't help but notice the jean shorts that barely passed her butt, or the tank top she was wearing. Her hair was now pulled into a ponytail high on her head. It wasn't until I saw the tired look in her eyes that I put together what he said about her house. I wanted to get up and hug her, let her know everything would be okay. That I had her back.

Or roof, as the case was.

I would have too, had her father, one of my closest friends, not beaten me to her.

"Hey, buttercup. Took you longer than I thought. Your cousins finish up?"

I watched her throat as she swallowed. "Yeah, they left just a few minutes after you. I wanted to clean out the fridge though. I hope you don't mind, but I brought some of the freezer stuff that was still semi-frozen. I was hoping you could help me get it all out of my car."

Marcus turned the grill down and closed the lid. "Sure. Oh, sorry. Ang, this is Jace. My friend from the corps I was telling you about."

I pushed to stand up, moving the ice pack onto the table. Her eyes caught it and I saw the question and concern burning in her eyes.

"Hey, Angela." I reached over and shook her hand. "Didn't recognize you all grown up." That was an understatement.

She rubbed her lips together, trying to keep back a smirk. I could still taste those lips on mine.

"Jace. Nice to see you again. Is your leg okay?"

"Yeah, just stiff from sitting on a plane all day." I waved to the house. "Should we grab that food before it thaws all the way out?"

"Yes, please." Angie spun on her heels and walked quickly away.

I looked up at Marcus, waiting for him to follow. Instead, he just stood there, watching me. "What?"

"Nothing." He shook his head, in a way that looked like he was telling himself he was crazy.

He wasn't. But I sure was. Hell, I nearly had a fling with my best friend's daughter. I still wanted her too, despite their relationship.

I followed them both out, racking my brain for what the right course of action to take here was. I mean, obviously I kind of already stuck us down the path of pretending my tongue wasn't down her throat just this morning, or last night. Or every time I closed my eyes.

Yeah, he didn't need to hear about all the fantasies I'd been having all day about his daughter.

Angie led us toward the driveway, where a dark red Hyundai Tucson sat. Right next to Marcus' old beat-up blue Ford truck. She pushed a button on her key fob and the trunk opened. She stepped to the side, while Marcus dove in and grabbed a large box. I watched her from behind his back. She was purposely not looking at me.

"I'll put these in the freezer. Jace, why don't you help Ang take her bags to her room." He turned and winked at me. "You could probably use the movement again."

I slapped his back. "Har, har. Maybe you should get one of those lifts to take your old butt up and down the stairs."

He gave a whole body, happiest man in the world laugh, as he walked away.

"Why do you need the movement? Is your leg okay?"

My head snapped back at the soft voice. I glanced back toward the house, making sure he was gone. Almost. Close enough to it.

"It's fine. It was stiff from being cramped on a plane for a few hours."

She gave me a sad sigh, then turned to walk around to one of the side doors. "You should have taken the first-class seat. There was more leg room."

I followed her, reaching out for her hand. "Hell, no. Besides, it sounds like you had a full day on your hands. You needed the time."

She nodded and pulled her hand back.

I sighed and watched as she grabbed the same duffle off the back seat. "How bad is it?" I needed to know.

Her eyes looked from me to the house, where her dad had disappeared into, then came back to me. Her sand dune eyes were starting to look a little muddy. Angie knew I wasn't talking about her house, but she chose to answer as though I was.

"Dad said it depended on supplies for how long it takes to fix the roof." She mumbled a few curses about her neighbors.

I followed her lead, personally preferring a different topic, but this would have to do for now. At least she was talking to me. I grabbed the two bags out of the back, and she pushed a button to close it.

"I'm sure it will be done in no time. I'll fix it as fast as I can, I promise."

She gave a huff, only half amused, and walked back into the house. She didn't speak again until we reached the top landing. Her eyes took in my leg, a worry crossing her beautiful face before she shook it off.

"I take showers in the morning. So, unless you sleep late, or wake up early…"

"I prefer showering at night." I cut her off.

She pressed her eyes closed, the tiniest whimper coming out, as she opened her bedroom and walked in. I was right there with her. Knowing she was going to be showering every morning, right across the hall from me, was going to be very difficult.

I dropped the bags on her bed and grabbed her waist, pulling her to me. I may have been a little desperate in the move, she yelped and glanced at the door.

"Tell me what to do, Angie. I'm drowning here. This was the last thing I expected."

Still keeping her eyes from mine, she put her hands softly on my chest. I didn't know if it was to maintain the distance or because she didn't know what to do with them.

"What did you expect, then?"

I closed my eyes and cursed at myself. She had that voice again, the one that said she didn't understand why I wanted her so much. I heard it many times last night, I just hadn't known for sure what it was. Marcus had mentioned more than once over the years how he worried about her self-confidence. I vaguely remembered something to do with a prick of an ex when she was younger.

I tipped her chin up, needing her to see the truth in my eyes. "I expected to call you tonight, to talk with you. I expected to ask you to go to dinner with me sometime over the next few days, when you weren't so busy getting ready for school. I expected to see you, a lot."

The tiniest of smiles wanted to come out. "And now?"

I sighed and dropped my head to hers. "And now, I still want all that. But I don't know what to do. Never in my wildest dreams did I think you would be my best friend's daughter."

Angie laid her head on my chest, and I wrapped my arms all the way around her. "Why did you say your name was Jason?"

I chuckled softly. "I don't know. It kind of just came out. Jason is my name. During basic, it got shortened and it stuck. Angie."

She tipped her head up, putting her chin on my chest. "Only my dad calls me Angela, and not even all the time. I usually go by Ang or Angie."

Unable to hold back anymore, I lowered my head and brushed her lips with mine. She slowly lifted onto her toes, pressing for more. Her lips were just beginning to part when we heard her dad call from the bottom of the stairs.

"Dinner's ready!"

Angie jumped back, as though she were surprised. She wasn't the only one that momentarily forgot he was still down there. Or even existed. She cleared her throat and stepped away from me. I followed her out and down the stairs.

"How big was the tree?" I asked as we reached Marcus.

Angie snorted, partial amusement at my cover and partial annoyance. "Little over half my living room. My place may not be real big, but that tree sure was." She mumbled a few more choice curse words about her neighbors.

Marcus and I both laughed.

"Well, I'll check it out tomorrow. Do you mind if I head over while you are at that meeting?"

She shook her head and grabbed a stack of plates out of the cabinet, bypassing the paper ones Marcus had sitting on the counter. He just laughed as she scowled at him.

Dinner passed slowly. Dreadfully slow.

CHAPTER 7

Angie

How did this happen?

One minute, I was looking forward to hearing from this incredibly handsome and fun guy I met. Someone I really wanted to spend more time with. Something I hadn't felt in a really long time.

The next, I discover that he was my dad's best friend. Someone my dad had been raving about for years. Someone my dad was excited for me to meet - as a family friend, not as a possible romantic partner.

My dad had been lonely since he was forced to leave the military to raise me. He lost his wife, the love of his life, and the career he loved all at once. Dad loved being in the infantry. He loved his buddies. He loved the military. He still bled freaking khaki for crying out loud.

I knew he loved me too, which was why he took the hardship discharge. I could have lived with grandpa. Or with my Aunt Kathy and her family. But my dad didn't want me to live without both parents. No matter how long we both lived, I would never be able to show him just how grateful I was, and always would be, for the sacrifice he made for me.

Well, I guess there was one way. I couldn't be what took his only tie back to the life he led away from him. I wouldn't allow it.

I doubted he would care much about Jace and I being together, but what if it didn't work out? I could ruin that friendship for him. Dad was a bit protective of me, just like I was of him. I could never do that to my dad. I could never risk a relationship that had lasted for as long as it had, even through the distance and separate lives they'd both led.

So, instead, I brought them out another round of beers. And bottles of water. We ate dinner on the patio table. Dad made up some chicken and potatoes on the grill. I swear he used that thing more than he did the actual stove.

I half listened as the two reunited friends swapped stories about their time together, and buddies they had in common. Dad had done his best to keep in touch with most of them. His way of keeping that lifeline for himself open. That was how I saw it anyway. He just called it keeping tabs on his "boys."

"Haven't heard from Kirby in a while. How's he doing?" Dad asked, taking the water bottle I placed in front of him, instead of the third beer he had asked for.

Jason had been laughing when I did that, but his smile shrank fast at the question. "I thought you heard. Kirby drove over a mine, two or three years back. Mustang was next to him."

Dad cursed softly and set the water back down slowly. "Mustang told me a little about how he ended up in the chair. He wasn't ready to talk about the rest yet. Makes sense."

Jason cleared his throat awkwardly. "Yeah. They uh, were stuck a ways from base. I read the report. Mustang held him while he took his last breath. For a while there, we weren't sure if Mustang would pull through. Those two were nearly inseparable in life." It was silent for a few minutes, both of them lost to sad memories.

"Why *Mustang?*" I asked, trying to lighten the mood. They both chuckled so it must have helped a little.

Dad grinned, it wasn't the completely happy one he had been wearing, but it was better. "Chris "Mustang" Curtis. He was obsessed with Mustangs. Pictures of them everywhere."

"Lucas "Kirby" O'Reilly had dark red hair, a round face, and lived for playing video games. When he wasn't working, he was playing." Jason added softly.

"Did you two have nicknames?"

Dad blushed and took a drink to hide his grin.

"I was mostly referred to as Jace, but a few liked to call me Bob the Builder. Mostly your dad." Jason chuckled, crossing his right leg over his left knee. He grimaced but tried to hide it. He kind of sucked at it.

"Dad?" I turned to him, trying not to think about Jason and his thigh. Or the way I would have loved to massage it for him. Which would most definitely lead to other things.

My dad scratched his jaw, which was getting a bit of a stubble with the late hour. Even that hair was coming out grayer now.

"I, uh, was called Joel from time to time."

Jason snorted. My dad rolled his eyes. "It was a little more often than that, Cap."

Dad reached a hand over to smack him, but Jason leaned far enough back that the half-hearted attempt passed.

"Why Joel?" That name wasn't even a real nickname.

Dad sighed, caving in. "Joel was the main character in an old movie."

I gave him a yeah and nod.

"*Risky Business* came out when we were kids. Your dad had a rep for being a bit risky when it came to missions."

I frowned and looked at my father. He raised his hands in surrender.

"I had the balls to go in when others didn't." I kept a very unhappy look on my face. He dropped the casual attitude about it and leaned across the table and grabbed my hands. "I was fine, wasn't I? They were calculated risks, and people needed help."

I rolled my eyes, shaking my head with it. "No wonder mom was always ticked at you."

Dad chuckled. "Yeah, the lovely gossip grapevine was always faster than I was at talking." Dad's face fell just a smidge, but I knew that look. He was thinking about mom again now. That was always a dark pit he easily fell into.

I pushed away from the table and began to clear things up. "It's getting late. I'll clean up, you two can head up to bed."

Dad stood up and kissed my cheek. "Thanks, buttercup. I'll see you in the morning." He was smiling again, probably because he was getting away with not having to clean.

"You want some help?" Jason at least offered.

"I got it. Thank you though." I tried to give him an encouraging smile but didn't want to look at him. I'd avoided eye contact with him as much as possible all night.

"You sure?"

Dad put an arm around his shoulder and pulled him toward the door. "When a woman says they got it, leave it be. Especially that one."

Jason smirked at him. "Still as lazy as always when it comes to cleaning, I see."

Dad laughed and hugged his friend from the side, throwing a wink at me over his shoulder. Yep, dad was thrilled to have us here. He wasn't alone. I tried to talk him into selling the house and moving into something smaller, but he didn't want to. He said he wanted the space in case I ever needed to come home.

Guess it was coming in handy this week.

I took my time washing the dishes by hand, then wiping down the counters and the patio table. I even swept the kitchen floor. Jason wasn't kidding, dad didn't like to clean. I always did what I could when I came over.

And I may have also been putting off going upstairs.

There were only three actual bedrooms in this house. I knew which one was Jason's without having to ask.

When I had nothing left to do, that wouldn't be obvious that I was procrastinating, I finally turned off the lights and locked up the house. I took the stairs slowly, quietly. Not wanting to draw attention to myself. I kept my eyes on the floor, pretending this was any other night, and no one of interest was in the room I was about to pass.

Unfortunately, that meant I didn't see the dark hole where a door should have been. As soon as I was directly in front of it, a figure popped out, put a hand around my mouth and pulled me in, closing the door in front of me.

I screamed, but it was muffled by the very large, very rough, hand.

"Shh, sweetheart, it's just me."

I stopped trying to scream and worked to slow my breathing back down. He slid his hand off my mouth and moved his arms around my waist. I shivered when he started kissing my neck.

"What are you doing, Jason?" I whispered. Even my voice was shaking.

"I can't stop thinking about you. You looked so beautiful in the moonlight. Your laugh fills me in a way nothing ever has. It took all I had to not touch you tonight."

My body melted into his, without permission, and I leaned against him. His grip grew tighter, like he was trying to weld our bodies together.

"Jason. We can't do this."

"Why?"

"Because that man down that hall hasn't been this happy in a long time. He is excited that you are finally here. He is happy to have that connection to his old life again. He lost more than just my mother. He lost his dreams. He lost… everything."

I squeaked as he roughly spun me around and backed me against the door. "Not everything. He had what was most important to him. And that will always be you."

"I know that. But that doesn't change how lonely he has been." When did my hands end up behind his head, playing with his hair? Jason's eyes closed as he soaked in the moment, enjoying the feeling. Which made me grip his hair tighter. I liked that he enjoyed my touch so much. With a low growl, his eyes opened and met mine, only seconds before he crashed his lips into mine.

He kept one hand on my back, the other slid down and lifted my leg up. I wrapped it around his leg, just like he wanted. His hand then began to climb up, under my tank top.

His kisses moved down my neck, the same time his hand dipped under the bra. I was shivering for a whole new reason now.

"Jason?" I whispered. He pressed harder into me, from all areas. "Jason." It was more of a moan than a question that time. Before I knew it, my top was on the floor and his lips were back on mine.

Jason lifted me up just enough that I could wrap my legs around his waist. He kept me pressed against the door for balance, while he took advantage of the missing clothes. I stopped trying to gain his attention, and enjoyed the attention he was giving my body.

Moments later, he was laying us carefully on the bed, the rest of our clothes having already been lost in the process.

"Jason, wait." I struggled with myself, but I managed to put a hand up between us. "My dad."

He pushed through my hand with ease, since it had no strength behind it, and kissed me slowly. "One night. One night to finish what we started in that airport. One night to satisfy our need for each other. Just give me one night, Angie."

His eyes were pleading, desperate. I nodded my agreement. He didn't even pause, just picked up where he left off.

A few minutes later, he started to move away. I grabbed the thick muscles on his arms. Like hell he was moving away right now.

He chuckled and kissed me again. "I'm not going far. Just grabbing something I picked up earlier, in hopes of seeing you soon."

I giggled. "You don't need it. I'm clean, and on the pill."

He growled and began sucking on my neck again. "I don't play around like most of the others did. I'm clean, too. Are you sure about this?" His words were mumbled like someone talking with their mouth full.

"Hell, yes." I moaned. I was starting to think he was part vampire. I'd be good with that. Then again, I'd be good with just about anything at the moment. Especially if Jason was the one doing it to me.

We both got what we needed, then I laid in his sweaty arms, our breathing still heavy. The last thing I was aware of was him kissing my forehead. For the second night in a row, I slept in his arms. At least the bed was more comfortable than the airport floor.

I woke up the next morning, the sun barely beginning to peek through the blinds, to soft kisses moving along my neck. I laughed as I blinked my eyes open. Jason slowly moved over me again and turned those kisses into more.

"Just one night, huh?" I teased him as he looked down at me.

He shrugged. "As long as you are in my bed, I am not going to be able to resist touching you." His hand grazed down the side of my face, and then down my neck. "Or kissing you." He softly kissed me. "Or…" My eyes closed and a moan slipped out my lips as he pressed deeper into me.

He dropped down next to me a few minutes later, a tired, but triumphant, grin on his face. We just laid there quietly, until we heard movement on the stairs. Dad was awake and headed down.

I sighed and sat up. "I need to get ready for work."
Jason sat up behind me and kissed my shoulder. "I will check out your house today. Just send me the address."

I nodded but didn't move. I just sat there, holding the sheet over my chest. Jason moved enough to place one leg on each side of me, then wrapped his arms around me from behind. I was grateful he didn't try to make me any more promises. We both knew what this was. And we both knew this was as far as we could ever go together.

Eventually, I pushed off the bed and slid my clothes back on. He kissed me one more time, then I fled to my room, then to the bathroom.

Half an hour later, I walked into the dining room. Dad had made pancakes, and both men were just sitting down to eat. Dad handed me a plate, already set up with pancakes and a few strawberries. I kissed his cheek and sat down to join them.

"What are your plans for today, buttercup?"

I picked up the syrup and basically dumped it on. "I have a staff meeting I have to get too soon, then I'll mostly work in my classroom after that. I am swinging by the pharmacy later. Did you need any more vitamins?"

I giggled at the look on his face. He hated taking vitamins. But he was getting older, and his doctor and I ganged up on him.

He growled playfully. "Only if the old man next to you has to take them too."

"Nah. He's not as old as you. We'll give him a few more years before we start harping on him."

Jason reached under the table and squeezed my knee. Dad just laughed.

"What do you need to get? You feeling alright?"
I cleared my throat awkwardly. I shouldn't have mentioned anything. "I, uh, called in a refill on my epi pen."

Jason's hand squeezed my knee tighter.

My dad's fork slowly lowered, one of his eyebrows going up. It was really not fair that I couldn't do that.

"Why?" Apparently his brain was working in slow motion this morning.

"It wasn't a big deal, daddy."

He cursed and dropped his fork on his plate. "What happened?"

"The waiter accidentally brought me a cherry coke at dinner the other night. I had the pen out before anything could really happen."

He gave me that look that called BS.

I sighed. "Fine, my eyes went a bit blurry, and I started coughing. My friend found the pen for me and stabbed me with it. All of it took less than two minutes from the moment I realized why it tasted different. Okay?"

I got up and moved to sit on his lap, giving him a hug. "I'm alright. I promise."

My dad just held me tight in response. After a minute or two, he sniffled, trying to act all manly, and I moved back to finish eating.

"We are meeting your cousins at your place later. Hopefully by the time you get home we will have a plan in place."

"Okay. I know you will have other calls coming in too. They can go first. I'm sure many of them are having to live with a hole in their roof. Not like me." I winked at my dad, and he chuckled.

"We'll see what comes in." We both knew that wasn't what would happen. I would always be the top priority to him.

I finished eating and got up to clean up the dishes. Jason stopped me this time. "Unlike your father, I *do* know how to clean."

"I don't have to take this abuse. At least I cooked." He pushed back from the table and stood up. His tone said he was offended, but the giant grin on his face said otherwise. He gave me another hug and kissed my head. "I'm going to go make a few calls. Have a good day, buttercup."

"You too. Be safe." I kissed his cheek back.

I barely had time to set the plates down before my back was against the counter, and the plates completely forgotten about. Jason had one hand on my lower back, pressing me against him. I wasn't exactly pushing him away either. My senses didn't come back until I felt his hand sliding down the back of leggings, following the inseam. I started to pull away, but stopped when he dropped his head to mine.

"I don't think I will ever get that memory of you gasping for air out of my head."

I closed my eyes. "Not exactly a good memory for me either. I hadn't planned on telling him. I knew he would take it hard."

"That was how your mom died, right?"

I nodded and leaned back enough to look into those chocolatey eyes. "Yes. She had the same allergy."

His hand slid down further, gripping me tight. I had to bite my lip to keep back the embarrassing sounds that I did *not* need my father to hear echo from the kitchen.

"I can understand why that would scar him. He is still taking her death hard."
"I know." I moved my arms to wrap around his neck in a hug, he buried his face in mine. "We said we weren't doing this again."

"I know." He sounded like pouting toddler.

My small laugh came out on its own. He pinched my butt in retaliation. Then sighed and released me, stepping back.

"My brain knows what we agreed on. But it doesn't feel right to not be able to touch you whenever I want."

I straightened my clothes and, once again, refused to meet his eyes. I was a crappy liar, no one believed me. Ever. This was my only chance to try.

"It's a habit. I'm sure we will break it. We just have to get used to it." It was far from a habit. And I could tell from the way his body tensed up that he didn't agree either. "I need to go. I'll see you later."

I pulled my hand back as he tried to grab it again and walked toward the living room. I grabbed my purse and half ran out the door. As soon as I was in the car and out of the driveway, I called Whit. I needed someone to talk to, someone to help me clear my head.

"Hey, about time you called. Did you get home before the storm hit?" The background noise died out as she left the room she was in.

"No. I got delayed in the airport. I didn't get home until yesterday afternoon."

"Wow. That must have been boring."

"Yes and no. That's actually why I'm calling." As I drove toward the school, the roads mostly cleaned up now, I filled her in on the whole debacle.

"So, let me get this straight. You get stuck in an airport for the night. Meet a hot guy. Win some money. Make out with said hot guy. He saves your life and upgrades you to first class. Then come home and find out he is your dad's best bud from the Army."

"Marines."

"Whatever. Sheesh. I miss all the good stuff. No, you cannot have another bag of fruit snacks, you already ate four. You want fruit so bad, grab an apple!"

I laughed. "Carolyn is still stuck on those fruit snacks, huh?"

Whit growled out a whine. "Yes."

"Why don't you just stop buying them?"

"I did. But she has her father wrapped around her little finger."

She could mope all she wanted. I knew it was fake. Whit loved how much Allen was whipped by both his girls.

"What do I do, Whit?"

"Well, it's a crappy place to be, but it sounds like he may be just as torn up about this as you are. Just do it. Get it out of your system. Maybe that would help."

I pulled into my normal parking spot at the school and just stared at the sky, thinking back on last night, and this morning.

"You already did, didn't you?"

"Maybe."

She laughed. "I know it has been a while for you, but there ain't no such thing as maybe. Either you did, or you didn't. Which is it?"

"Did." I sighed in defeat. "Twice. He sort of ambushed me in the hall last night and pulled me into his room. I fell asleep in his bed after, so he sort of woke me up this morning too."

Whit whistled. "Hot."

"He also basically attacked me after breakfast. As soon as my dad left the room."

"Girl! Why are you even struggling? Man, if I were there right now, I would smack you!"

"Why?" I saw others pulling in and waved hi to them.

"Because he likes you!"

"Yeah, but what about my dad?"

"So, what about him? He wants you to be happy, doesn't he?"

"Yes, but what if it doesn't work out? Dad might lose one of his best friends."

I could tell Whit was losing her patience with me. "Angela, darling. Stop thinking about the negatives." I heard a crash and she groaned.

"Jason and I both agreed this was for the best."

"No. I think you told him, and he agreed just to make you happy. Look, wait it out for a few weeks. See if things cool down. If they don't, then you two need to talk about this, for real this time." She growled out Carolyn's name. "I gotta go. Love ya."

I giggled. "Love you, too. Good luck!"

I turned the car off and climbed out of my car. I detoured by my classroom to drop my things off before the meeting. As soon as I flipped on the lights, I looked around and took a deep breath. Home. It felt good to be home.

At least one of them was still in one piece.

CHAPTER 8

Jason

"My girl get off okay?"

I choked on the water I had just taken a drink of and looked up at Marcus' amused expression. I leaned forward from where I was sitting on the couch, setting the bottle back on the coffee table.

"Maybe we need to have your ears checked too. Did Angela leave for work okay?"

I cleared my throat and wiped my mouth. "Yeah. She left not long after you went up." I creased my eyes and studied him. "How are you?"

He plopped down across from me, sitting in an armchair. "I'm fine. Why?"

"You looked upset about her having to use the Epi pen."

He rubbed a hand down his face. "It doesn't happen often, but when it does, it never fails to scare the hell out of me. I can't lose her too. And definitely not in the same way I lost her mother."

"I didn't remember Marta being allergic to anything."

"We didn't know." He leaned forward, his elbows on his knees. "I don't care for cherries myself, so we never had them. We didn't know that her father was allergic to them as well. No one bothered to have the kids tested. His was only a mild irritation. They assumed it would be the same for the kids, if they had any reaction at all. Then, one day, her and Ang were out to breakfast. She picked up the strawberry syrup and drowned her pancakes in it. The way she always did. The way they both do. Turns out, it wasn't strawberry. Ang had to sit there and watch her mother's face swell up. By the time the ambulance got there, it was too late. I had Ang tested the minute I got home. And then made her promise to always carry the pen on her. It happened in front of me twice. Her eyes always go first. She was lucky she had already made that friend. What would have happened if she had been alone?" His voice cracked at the end.

I gave him a minute to pull himself back together. At least, that was the impression I gave him. I hadn't known about her eyes. From the outside, she almost looked normal. The swelling had barely started, along with the couple coughs, by the time I pushed the medicine into her.

Marcus stood back up and slapped my shoulder. "Come on. Let's get you to her house. Kyle and Kent will be meeting us there."

I stood up and followed him out to my car. "And they are?"

"My sister Kathy's boys. I got the girl, and she got two sons. Ever since she started dating Karl Kennedy, she has had an obsession with the letter K." He shook his head and sank into the front seat of the compact car I picked up. "We need to get you a bigger car."

I laughed. "It's on my list of things to do. This was all they had available yesterday."

He nodded. The only talking we did over the next fifteen minutes was him giving me directions. We pulled up in front of an all-white small house, with a black truck parked in the driveway. I built houses for a living, and I still couldn't tell you the difference between a bungalow and a house. Of course, I could say the same thing about a cottage too.

The place was cute. Except for the large tree sitting in the middle of the lawn, and the blue tarp on top of the roof.

I stepped out of the car and gave a low whistle. "Small hole, huh?"

He shrugged and closed the door. "Yep. And that is exactly what I will keep telling her. Ang bought this place, on her own, not long after she started teaching. It was a hellhole. But she got a good deal. We worked on it together for nearly a month. A family project so to speak. This place is her baby."

"Not just hers." A deep voice came from the house. "It's all of ours. We put our sweat, blood, and tears into this place."

I looked up and saw two young men coming out of the house. They were both a bit on the lanky side, but their struts said they had some muscle. They had the same sandy brown hair as Marcus, but their skin was a shade lighter and their eyes more on the bluer side.

"Jace, these are my nephews. Kyle and Kent."

I shook their hands. "You guys twins?"

They chuckled. "No, but we get that a lot. I'm older by two years." Kyle held up two fingers.

"Kyle was in the same grade as Ang when we moved home. He kept an eye on her for me."
"Pretty sure you got that backward, Uncle Marcus. I do believe it was her that ratted me out. Just about every week." He played up the offense.

"And you deserved it every time." Kent smacked him on the back of the head. "It's nice to meet you, Jace. Uncle Marcus told us you were coming."

I nodded, shaking his offered hand. Knowing the chatterbox, Marcus probably told them a lot.

"The boys work for me. Their dad never did like getting his hands dirty, but these guys can't sit still behind a desk either."

"Nope. Although pop still tries to push us in his direction once in a while." Kyle rolled his eyes.

"And which direction is that?" I asked.

"Accounting." They both gave dramatic shivers. Honestly, we all did.

"Alright, let's get up there and see what we are working with. We've had a few people calling already this morning, wanting us to come out. We're going to be busy."

I followed Marcus to the boys' truck, where I helped him pull out a ladder.

"How many people do you have working for you?"

"About a dozen most days. I've sent a few off to start giving estimates on those that called. They are decent enough with roofs, but not near as good as you. Which is why you will focus on Angela's place. As much as I love having her home again, she loves her little place."

He held the ladder, and I climbed up. Marcus followed quickly behind me. I walked along the edge of the roof, until I got to a part that felt a little sturdier. I moved the weights holding the tarp down and lifted it up. Then whistled again. It wasn't just the gaping hole, or the smaller ones spread out, or even the parts where shingles were coming off. It was the whole thing added up.

"She's going to need most of this roof replaced."

"You can't just patch it up?" Kyle asked from where he stood on the top rung of the ladder.

I shook my head, my eyes still taking it all in. "Not if you want it to last through another storm. The winds and rain alone would deteriorate the next one faster than you can say Oorah." I lowered the tarp and put the weight back on. "This is going to take a few days."

Marcus cursed and hit his knee. "Can you do it?"

"Sure. Won't be a problem. I'll need an extra set of hands on some days though. If it weren't for this thigh, I'd be good on my own."

Marcus nodded and waved toward Kyle. "He's been wanting to learn more about roofing. I was planning on giving him to you anyway. He might have to site hop some days, but, as I said the boy don't know how to sit still."

"That's fine." I rubbed my foot against a loose shingle. "Did you use clay?"

"Yeah. That was what was already here. We didn't have to update the whole thing, just part of it. What are you thinking in that big brain of yours?"

I squatted down, ignoring the pinch in my thigh, and moved some of the shingles around. "I'm thinking at least half her ceiling is going to need to be replaced. I didn't look close enough yet, but I'm thinking some of the ones you replaced had had leaks before that. The size of that tree down there is pretty big, but not big enough to do all this. I'm willing to bet a few of these beams were already rotten. I want to replace the whole thing. And then, maybe use steel shingles. They last longer and they will help keep the heat out, and her power bill down."

Marcus walked around the perimeter of the roof, bouncing lightly every now and then.

"You might be right." He rubbed a hand down his face. "Her insurance should pay out for most of this. Which should be enough for the materials."

Kyle snorted. "Not gonna charge your precious baby for manual labor?"

Marcus turned and glared at him. "Should I tell her you suggested that?"

Kyle paled. "Please don't. I like my balls where they are, thank you."

Kent roared with laughter from below.

"That's what I thought. Besides, you know Ang. She'll find a way to pay you back."

"True." He nodded.

Carefully, we climbed back down and gathered in a circle around the tree.

"What are your plans for this?" I pointed at the tree that offended Angie so much.

"I brought my chainsaw. I promised her yesterday I would cut it up and she could use it for firewood. The look on her face was a little creepy though." Kent shivered. "When Missy gets that look, I know I'm screwed."

"Missy?"
"His wife." Marcus walked around the tree, which was apparently on Angie's hit list, and went inside the house.

I followed him. "She'll have to repaint in here too."

It was hard to tell the original color of the walls, as it was so dark without power. But the water stains were obvious.

"Yep. And maybe some new drywall. I'm worried about mold."

"Once the ceiling is rebuilt, and the roofing done, I can hit this room from the inside."

"She'll probably help you. Girl has a talent with drywall." I lifted an eyebrow and he laughed. "She may not look it, but that daughter of mine has a wicked swing with a hammer. She used to work with me on weekends and during the summer. One year, one of her little friends even came to work with us. Nat studied architecture in college. She needed to intern for a class, so I brought her on."

"That was nice of you."

He walked into the kitchen and flipped a light switch on, but nothing happened. "We'll need to check her breaker box. Her neighbors have power, so she should too." Marcus sighed and led the way back out of Angie's house.

Kent was wielding the chainsaw, cutting up the tree. Kyle was grabbing the finished pieces and piling them up near the garage. We waited until they were done.

While Kent packed it up and put it away, Kyle came over to us.

"When do you want to get started?"

"First I need to get myself a truck. Pretty sure rental insurance doesn't cover construction sites." I turned to Marcus. "Do you need him elsewhere today? I don't know how long that will take."

Marcus checked his phone, scrolling through messages. "Yeah. We have three more houses being worked on today. While you go car shopping, we will spread out and see where we can help. Most of those are just basic roof repairs."

"Sounds good. Once I have the car taken care of, I will come back and get a closer look at the power and what supplies I will need."

Marcus put out his arm and I grasped it. "I can't tell you how happy I am that you are finally here, man."

I huffed in amusement and shook my head. "I am too. It feels good to be here. To be doing something." I wouldn't mention what I would rather be doing though. I was feeling pretty certain his daughter had more to do with my happiness at the moment than he did.

"That's a good sign. Maybe I can convince you to stick around a while."

It all depended on Angie.

Marcus loaded up with his nephews, and I got into my rental. Before they left, Marcus referred me to his dealership. It took me four hours of paperwork, but I finally got myself my first car. A black Dodge Ram. Enterprise was kind enough to come pick up their rental car from the dealership.

I swung through a drive thru for lunch and headed back to Angie's. It felt kind of nice to be driving my own car. All those winnings from the airport came in handy too. They were enough to pay a little over half the price of the car up front.

I walked around the back of her little house, searching for the breaker box. I paused and took in the view. I hadn't paid any attention when I was on top of the house earlier. She had her backyard outlined with a white wooden fence, about three feet high. She had a small seating area on a raised porch. Past the yard, was a drop off to another row of houses, and then the beach. I found the box near the patio. I flipped each of the switches and made sure they were firmly in the on position. When a patio light flickered on I figured it was working. With the easy part done, I walked back around and entered through the front door with the key Marcus handed me before we had all left earlier.

The interior of the house was decorated in earth tones and in a comfortable fashion. Or at least it would be. If it wasn't for the gaping hole in the ceiling. I walked around the living room, pressing on the walls. There were a few bubbles in some of the drywall, but the rest felt sturdy. There didn't look to be any other structural damage. Which was good.

Out of curiosity, I walked down the narrow hall. I found a guest bathroom and two guest bedrooms. Both made up with the basic furniture needs. They held abstract art paintings and continued with the earth tones. The last room was the largest. And the most colorful.

It had an ensuite bathroom, a small sofa to one side, near a dresser, and a large bed. The bed had a dark red comforter, with black flowers. The walls were mostly off-white. The wall behind the bed had black flowers and butterflies surrounding the headboard. As though they were sprouting and flying away from the bed.

I could picture Angie lying in the bed, sleeping. In my arms.

What I wouldn't give to wake up next to her every morning. I cleared my throat awkwardly and speed walked back down the hall. I needed to focus on my purpose there. Which wasn't making her mine.

I spent the next two hours on the roof, moving the tarp around, taking measurements, and making notes of all the supplies I would need.

CHAPTER 9

Angie

I didn't think about where I was going, until I pulled into my house. I must have driven on automatic pilot after I left the school. There was a large black truck sitting in my driveway, one I didn't recognize. Kyle drove a black Ford. But this one was not a Ford.

Cautiously, I stepped out of my car, grabbed my purse, and walked toward my house. As soon as I beeped the car lock, a head popped over the side of my roof.

Jason.

The relief was quickly followed by anxiety and a lot of nervous energy. My stomach even erupted in butterflies. When had that ever happened to me before? At least when it concerned a guy.

"Hey." I waved, feeling stupid. I had no real reason to be there. Was he going to think I came here to see him?

"Hey."

I walked toward him, feeling his eyes on me every step of the way. I climbed the ladder and stopped just enough to see what he was doing. My face fell as soon as I saw the roof without the tarp. What was left of it anyway.

My jaw dropped. "It killed my house."

Jason chuckled and walked over to me, squatting down in front of me. "No, it just banged it up a little. Let me cover this back up and I'll meet you inside."

I gave my roof one more sad look then climbed back down. I sat in my little dining area, listening to the sounds of him moving around. I mentally kicked myself when I noticed the slight limp as he joined me a few minutes later. I jumped up to go to him.

"Are you okay? Should you be up there doing all that? You could fall or hurt your leg worse! Maybe you should ask Ky…"

I couldn't blame him for cutting me off, but I could blame him for how he did it. And for how I reacted and how long it lasted.

It was him that picked me up and sat me on the counter.

And it was so not my fault my legs wrapped around him, or that my hands pushed his shirt up so I could feel that chest again. The sweatiness of it just made it better somehow.

He pulled away with a grin. "I'm fine. I've spent most of my life on top of houses."

"I know, but the military put you behind a desk for a reason. And if you get hurt up there because of me…" He kissed me again and laughed. I gave up on the argument. "We aren't supposed to be doing this."

"You are the one that is under *my* shirt this time."

"Yeah, but you are the one who kissed me."

He kissed my nose. "I can't help it. You were freaking out over nothing, and I wanted to make you feel better."

I tilted my head to the side as he trailed down my neck. My head rolled as he made his way around, until he made a full circle back to my lips.

"Better?"

"Ya huh." A sad sigh slipped out and he stopped. "This isn't helping. We're supposed to be taking a step back."

He raised his hands up, taking my blouse with him. He pulled it right over my head, then held his hands in surrender.

"Seriously?"

"You said to take a step back. That's what I did. Your shirt must have just gotten stuck to me. Dried sweat can be sticky."

It was really hard not to smile when he was grinning at me like that. "No, that's what happens when you hold the shirt in your fingers."

"I did no such thing." He shook his head, his eyes not leaving mine. "It must have just really wanted to come off. Would it make you feel better if mine came off too? It could probably use the break from all that sweat."

I didn't even have a chance to shout no, which I totally would have, before his shirt came off too. He dropped them both on the counter next to me, then stepped back between my legs.

"Still want me to take that step back?"

I gulped, my hands already moving all over his hard chest. "You are not playing fair." I mumbled against his lips, already wondering what that sweat tasted like.

"I know. I will play nice. I promise... Eventually."

I laughed as he began pushing my leggings down. I helped him with his jeans.

It wasn't long before we stood there, both of us panting. Him still firmly lodged in place.

"Jason."

"I know. I know. I won't apologize though. Every time I see you, I can't help but want to touch you. I've been thinking about you all day."

"Really? So, my roof is never going to get fixed then?"

He poked my side and I flinched away with a laugh. Carefully, he stepped back and reached to where I kept tissues on the counter. He softly cleaned us both up, then helped me get dressed again.

"So, what's the verdict on my house?"

He brushed my hair behind my ear. "You need a new ceiling. And most likely new drywall in the living room. I should have up top done by the weekend. Your dad said you are good with drywall. Maybe we can start that part on Friday afternoon, when you get home from work."

I couldn't help it; the stupid tears came out on their own. He pulled me in and held me while explaining why all that needed to be done. He told me all about Kyle helping him, even though my dad had other jobs going on at the same time. I forced myself to suck it up. My dad was spread thin as it was and was still trying to help me out. It would have been rude and ungrateful of me to get upset.

"I will get it done as fast I can, I promise."

Even though I didn't say how I felt, didn't mean Jason didn't know it. I chose not to think about why he was already so good at reading me.

I shook my head, clearing the dangerous thoughts out, and pushed away. "No. Just do the best you can. I don't want you to rush it and end up hurting yourself. I'm glad Kyle will be helping you. I'll feel really bad if you screw that leg up because of me."

"My leg is fine. The only reason the Marines didn't want me building any more houses was because I wouldn't be able to move as fast as the others if insurgents came again. I can move around fine. I am just still working the strength back up on it."

"Is there a way I can help?"

His eyes darkened and his grin grew. "Well, now that you mention it…"

I lifted a finger and pointed at him. "No. This was the last time. We can't keep doing this."

His grin fell and taking my heart with it. "I know. I know." Well, now he just sounded like a petulant teenager. He yanked his shirt off the counter and put it back on.

I should apologize, but I also needed to stand my ground. One of us had to be the strong one here. At least until whatever this was, wore off.

Once I was decent again, I picked my purse back up and we walked out.

"Did you trade in the rental you had?"

"No. I bought this truck today. Gotta have something reliable. Technically, this is my first car." He walked me to my car and opened the door for me.

"You've never had a car before?"

"Nope. If I needed anything, I borrowed one from the motor pool. Perks of being an officer. You have to remember, sweetheart, I've lived on military bases for nearly 30 years. I walked most places."

"Yeah, but those places weren't always small."

"No, but I didn't need much. I lived in the barracks, or in a tent." He shrugged. "I didn't need much."

My hand misbehaved and cupped his cheek. "This must be hard for you. Being out, being here."

He wrapped his calloused fingers around my wrist, then turned and kissed my palm softly, before lowering it back down. "Yes and no. Being here is surprisingly easy. I guess Cap was right, I just needed something to keep me busy." Stiffly, he leaned forward and kissed my forehead. "I'll see you at home."

I managed to hold the tears back until he could no longer see me. Space. We needed space. That was all.

While Jason showered that night, I made a pot of pasta for dinner. Thankfully, Dad had put some of the meat I brought over in the fridge, since it was nearly done defrosting anyway. I carefully spread butter over some bread, then lightly layered them with garlic powder, before putting the pan in the broiler.

Once those were in, I drained the noodles. By the time everything was done, dad was walking in from work, and Jason was headed down the stairs. Hair wet and smelling divine.

I only half listened as they talked shop during dinner. They were still talking and eating by the time I stood up and put my plate in the sink. I didn't exactly eat fast, but I didn't take my time either.

"I cooked. You clean." I told my dad, he laughed. "I've got work to do upstairs. I'll see you both in the morning." I gave dad a hug and nodded my head at Jason. What else could I do in front of my dad?

I laid on my bed and stared at the ceiling. I had no motivation to make lesson plans. I had no motivation to do anything. Eventually, I heard them both come up the stairs and go into their rooms. A few minutes later, my phone dinged.

Jason: Are you ok?

I snorted. Nope. Not in the least bit.

Me: Fine. How is your leg?
Jason: Fine. It could use a massage though…
Me: Nice try.
Jason: Sigh…worth a shot.
Me: Goodnight, Jason.

I silenced my phone and plugged it in. I ignored it when I heard the buzz. He was 14 years older than me. Why did I have to keep being the grown up?

The next morning, I was up and out the door before either of them came down for breakfast. When they both messaged to ask where I was, I told them I had to get to work. And that was how it ran the next few days. I left early every morning, and I came home in time for dinner every night. Then I hid in my room. I had no need to work from home, since I had plenty of time to do that at work.

Overall, I avoided my own house like the plague.

Until Friday, when I caved to the desire to see my house. I told myself it was only the need to check on it. It had nothing to do with anyone else who might be there. I pulled up a little after one, earlier than I was supposed to be there, hoping Jason and Kyle would be gone for lunch.

No such luck. The shiny black truck was sitting in my driveway. Maybe they took Kyle's truck to lunch.

I almost didn't beep my car to lock it, but I did anyway. I kept one eye on the roof, but no head popped out. Breathing a sigh of relief, I walked up my path, noticing that I needed to weed my flower bed soon. The door was unlocked, which sank my hopes of no one being there.

I walked in and looked up. Then I gasped. It was done. At least from the inside. There was even a new ceiling fan spinning slowly in the middle of it.

"Hey."

I turned toward the voice that I dreamed of every night. "Hey," I pointed up. "It looks good. How's the other side?"

Jason set down his measuring tape and walked closer, as though a magnet was pulling us together. "It's done. We put steel shingles on, which should help keep some of the heat out."

I squealed with excitement and jumped up, wrapping my arms around his neck. "Thank you!"

A part of me was expecting for it to not be done yet. Lady luck hadn't really been on my side lately.

His arm came around me, bracing me, then the other soon followed, holding me. The tension thickened in a heartbeat, and the hug I meant in gratitude quickly filled with longing. Neither of us let go.

"You're welcome." He mumbled into my neck. He squeezed one more time, when we heard the front door open, then let me go.

"Do I get a hug too?"

I laughed at my dorky cousin, as Jason and I parted, and turned to give him a hug. "Thank you, Kyle. I can't tell you both how grateful I am."

"Tired of your old man, already?"

I punched Kyle in the stomach with the back of my fist. "Never. I got the cool dad, remember?"

He grumbled. "Yeah, I know." Uncle Karl was nice, just a little on the boring side.

"We can start the drywall early. We should only need to do one wall. You still up for it?" Jason asked.

"Definitely. Who all is helping?"

"Just you two. I've got plans, so I can't come. For so little, you should be fine." Kyle chuckled softly.

With the wall, yes. With not getting distracted, no. I pushed those thoughts aside. "What are you doing?"

"Got a date." Kyle grinned like an idiot.

"Ya huh. Does this one have a name?"

"Har, har. Her name is… uh…" Jason and I both laughed. "Kelsey!" He snapped his fingers, then frowned. "Or was it Chelsea."

I shook my head at him and patted his shoulder. "You better figure it out before tonight."

He was still thinking hard as he said goodbye and took off to go help dad somewhere else. The door had barely closed behind him before two arms wrapped around me from behind.

"You've been hiding from me." He set his chin over my right shoulder.

"No, I've been forcing the space we both need."

"I don't need space. And I don't want space."

I sniffed and turned my head to face the opposite direction. I knew if I looked his way, it would be his fault for what happened next. "We've talked about this."

He grumbled out a curse word, or five, and pushed away from me. "Yeah. I need to go pick up a few things. I'll be back in an hour, then we can get started."

I barely had time to nod my head before he was gone.

Lovely, I hurt him again. That was his fault too. We both agreed on taking space. It was his fault he kept pushing it.

I changed to a pair of leggings and an old t-shirt. I searched through my cabinets for something to eat, settling on an old bag of chips. I was going to need to go shopping later today.

I heard the sounds of Jason's diesel truck pulling back into the driveway an hour later. Right on time. I had the door opened before he got there. While he brought the new sheets of drywall in, I popped off the outlet covers. Then I used the knife and started cutting along the lines he had already drawn. He was back a few minutes later, helping me remove it all carefully.

We put all three sheets in together, then started putting on the first mud coat. I started on the right, while he started on the left. When we got to the middle, he stood behind me and worked over my head. I elbowed him for being a brat, he smacked my butt. The teasing stopped fairly quickly after that.

All in all, it only took us two hours to get that much done.

"How long do we need to wait before doing the next coat?"

He set his tools down and brushed his hands off on his jeans. "An hour or two should be fine. Are you hungry? We can go grab a bite to eat while we wait?"

I literally had to bite back the enthusiastic yes. For one, I was starving. For two, I just wanted to be with him.

"What about my dad?"

"He knows we are working on your walls today. He's not expecting me back anytime soon. I, uh, told him I might just work on it through the night." I lowered my eyebrows at him, and he laughed, raising his hands up. "I was talking about the wall. Obviously."

"Uh huh. Sure. Just let me clean up. There is a nice little Cuban place down the street."

"It's a date." He raised his hands again when I playfully scowled at him again.

As soon as we were out the door, he took my hand, kissed the back of it, and then held it while we walked. At the restaurant, he held my chair for me, and then continued holding my hand while we ordered and talked. And I let him. It was really hard not to. It was like we slipped right back into our own little bubble from the airport.

Just us. No one else existed.

By the time we got back to my place, the first coat was dry. Not everyone could get it to dry so quickly, only the pros, which Jason obviously was.

Starting on our own ends again, we started scraping over the mud, making sure it was smooth. This time, when we both reached the middle, his hand rubbed my back softly. We mostly worked in silence, as we put the next layer on. He asked a few questions about work, and my plans for the first week.

When we finished the last bit, a few hours later, I fell to the floor, completely exhausted,

Jason set his tools down more gracefully then I had. It was a good thing he had covered my floors before working on my ceiling and roof. Mine may have splattered some. He squatted down next to me, one hand on my back.

"Are you alright?"

"Yeah." I pushed out the breath, then pushed myself to stand back up. "Just tired. I haven't done this in a while, and uh, I haven't slept all that great this week."

He put his hands in his pocket and forced himself to take a step back. "Maybe sleeping in your own bed tonight will help."

Sure, if that was the problem. I met his eyes for a second, then turned, trying to blink the tears away. I walked down the hall, toward my room. I needed a minute to myself. I needed to breath.

I pushed the door closed behind me but didn't wait to see if it latched. Then dropped down the middle of my bed.

I jumped when I heard his deep chuckle. I lifted my right arm off the bed and flipped him off, which seemed to make him laugh harder. I groaned and buried my face in a pillow.

I was vaguely aware of my tennis shoes being untied and pulled off my feet.

"The wall…"

"Will take a few hours to dry. You can rest."

I mumbled out okay, not sure he caught it though. I groaned as he started rubbing my legs. Little by little, he rubbed up my thighs, one large hand on each leg. When he reached my back, he stopped, and I whined. Which made him laugh.

"Hold on, sweetheart. I'm coming back."

"You better be." I had my eyes closed and my head turned to the side. I was relaxed.

I heard a few thunks, probably his shoes. Good. I didn't want those suckers on my bed. I felt the bed dip down on one side, and then the other. I felt a small weight over my butt, then his hands began rubbing up and down my back.

I moaned, he pressed deeper.

As he moved up, he pushed my shirt with him. "Lift up, sweetheart." He whispered softly.

I did as he said and let him pull my shirt off. I sighed happily once the sweaty thing was gone. He chuckled and kissed me between my shoulder blades, his hands rubbing my shoulders. After a few minutes, when they were putty in his hands, he started working his way back down. I noticed but was passed caring when my bra clasp released.

Jason's hands worked up and down my back, slowly getting more and more of my sides. I felt whisper soft kisses moving along my spine. His hands slowly pushed their way up again, no longer on my back. I arched, almost like a cat, my butt pressing against him. I felt something lovely back there.

His hands slid back down, until they were on my waist, pushing my leggings down with them. He lifted one leg at a time, with only one hand, the other was still rubbing my back, until he had my pants gone. With both hands, he rubbed up again, only one strayed way off my back this time. I arched again and felt him even better. There was almost nothing between us.

"Jason. Please." I whimpered. I needed him. I missed him. I didn't care that I was going back on what I said. I didn't care that I was being a hypocrite.

At least he didn't make me ask again. Or beg for that matter. I wasn't above it. I lifted my hands and gripped the bedding under me, as he gave me what I desperately needed. It was kind of nice not having to worry about my dad hearing me. Jason seemed to like that too.

His head hit the pillow next to me a few minutes later, I crawled over and collapsed onto his arm.

"Best massage, ever." I yawned.

His laugh started out small, then grew as he held me closer so I wouldn't move away. He took a deep breath to steady himself, I tipped my head back to look at him. I scowled at him for laughing at me. He wasn't fazed. Then he kissed me, and I wasn't scowling anymore.

He tried to keep it small, but I kind of missed kissing him. I put my hand on the back of his head and pulled him back down. Forcefully. At least he was good at following orders.

It wasn't long before he had me on my back.

We spent the next few hours like that. Sleeping on and off, and then *sleeping* on and off. We both knew this really had to be it. With me out of my dad's house again, we would hardly see each other. Which should help keep this insane need we both had at bay. In time, it would fade to nothing.

I blinked my eyes open when the sun rudely woke me. I looked around the room, confused, when I noticed that I was alone.

CHAPTER 10

Jason

I didn't fall asleep when Angie did. Instead, I just laid there and held her. That massage worked out better than I had planned. I was only trying to show her that I cared about her. Not only for the physical release, but emotionally.

I just got a little distracted along the way. As did she. Apparently.

I pushed myself from the bed, using all my willpower to move away from her. The only other way I knew how to show her how I felt, was to finish the job *for her*. I went back to the living room, back to where we left off, wearing only my boxers. The mud was dry now, so I went ahead and started working on the corners. Once that was done, I went back to check on her.

The blanket had come down, so I tiptoed over to fix it. She mumbled my name in her sleep, and I caved. I ended up waking her up, just to knock her out again. When I was sure she was back under, I went back to the living room, back to work.

It was odd. My longest relationship lasted six months. Back when I was stationed in Germany, it was more of an in between posts post, I dated a girl named Monika. She was spunky. She was smart. She was fun. I stayed with her on my nights off. Even during our prime, I never had this deep of a craving for her. Not the way I did for Angie.

The day I found out I was being transferred we said our goodbyes. She wrote a couple times, and I replied when I could. She got married about a year later, and soon after started popping out kids. We were still friends. It never bothered me that she moved on.

Would I be able to say the same about Angie?

I was pretty sure I knew the answer to that already. And it scared the hell out of me. Especially since she was in this weird place of pushing me away, but then pulling me back in. Not that I had helped with that much.

Maybe I should show her how much I cared about what she wanted by backing off?

Just the thought of it was like a knife to the chest. It hurt a whole hell of a lot more than getting shot and falling off that skeleton of a house had.

After the fill coat, I washed up, then climbed back in bed with Angie. She rolled back into my arms. Her bare chest hitting mine.

I woke her up again. This time we both slept after.

I woke up a few hours later when my phone buzzed on the floor. I blinked a few times, clearing my eyes. Then reached down to my jeans, which I had dropped on the floor with my shoes, before straddling her legs for that massage. They weren't all that flexible and had tried to limit me on what I could do for her.

Cap: How's that wall coming along? You two need some help?

I cursed and shot up. I froze when I heard soft moaning coming from behind me. I turned and kissed her head, rubbing a gentle hand down her hair. She settled, I sighed.

Me: Almost done. Thought I'd take a nap. Just need to apply the final coat and sand.
Cap: Angela?
Me: Been asleep for hours. Didn't want to wake her.
Cap: Good call. She's snarly when she's tired.

I laughed as quietly as I could. To me she wasn't snarly, but then again, I didn't give her a chance to be. She never complained when I woke her up. Not that I was going to tell him that though.

Me: That would have been good to know last night.
Cap: You good, or do you need help?
Me: I'm good. You can help her paint later.

I shoved myself off the bed, hissing softly at the pinch. I may have overdone it this week. I needed to start exercising my leg regularly again.

I pulled my clothes back on, in case her father decided to come by anyway, and hobbled my way back into her living room. I stretched my leg out, running in place for a minute. It helped a bit.

The sun was higher when I felt two arms wrap around my waist. Lips pressing against my back.

"Have you been working all night?"

I lowered my arm and pulled her in front of me, trapping her between my arms. "On and off."

She did her version of lifting an eyebrow at me, which always made it hard for me not to laugh. I didn't need Cap to tell me that was a bad idea. It was obvious she did not like being laughed at. But it also wasn't hard to change her mind. When she let me, that is.

"As in, when you weren't molesting me in my sleep, you were out here."

I winked and kissed her head.

"Did you sleep at all?"

I leaned down enough to put my drywall knife down. Then wrapped her in both my arms. "I slept. With you. Frequently. I just got up to work in small shifts."

"How was that good for you?"

I shrugged softly, not wanting to risk loosening my grip on her. "I'm helping you. That is good for me."

"Awe." She went on her toes, so I lowered down, meeting her halfway.

I was thinking about carrying her back to that bed when I heard a truck pull up. Angie dropped back down with a resigned sigh. She knew that sound as well as I did, if not better.

"Did you know he was coming?"

"Technically, no. But I had a feeling. He messaged this morning and asked if we needed help. I told him no."

She stepped away and patted her shirt down. "But he will come anyway."

"You might want pants on before he comes in."

She cursed, looked down, cursed again, and then ran out of the room. I leaned to the side and enjoyed the view more than I probably should have. I went to her front door and opened it, right as Marcus started unlocking it with his key.

"Just couldn't help yourself, could you?"

He chuckled and lifted up a white rectangular box. "I come bearing gifts."

I sniffed and smiled. "Smells good."

"Where is my monster?"

"Right here. Give me that and I will let you enter." Angie told him with a straight face. She took the box, which he gave up willingly, and kissed his cheek. "Thank you, daddy." She sang.

While she sat down and started eating, Cap and I picked up the knives and finished the last coat. While it dried, we ate the donuts. Well, what was left of them at any rate. I loved that this woman didn't care about how much she ate. She enjoyed her food the way it was meant to be enjoyed.

"We'll come by tomorrow and finish sanding this down." Marcus told Angie. "You can paint on Monday or wait until next Saturday."

"Sounds good. Thank you for your help."

"Hey! I did all the work." I mocked the offense. They both laughed.

Angie walked over and went on her toes to kiss my cheek. "Thank you, Jace. I appreciate all the work you did."

Well, now I just felt awkward. Which her dad found funny. My heated cheeks weren't helping any.

I collected all my tools and loaded up the truck. Marcus and I headed back to his place, where I took a long overdue shower, then joined him on the patio.

The place was quiet. Too quiet. I kept shifting, not sure what to do with myself.

"Too much down time already?" He didn't even have to look at me. He just knew.

"Yes. How do you get used to it?"

"Practice. We can pull out some cards if you want. Watch a movie. But you're not leaving. You need to adjust to having more down time."

I grumbled my displeasure at that. We spent our afternoon playing cards. That night, we ordered a pizza and watched a movie. And, like the old men we apparently were, we went to bed early.

Sunday followed the same pattern. We went and sanded down Angie's wall in the morning, which didn't take long at all. Angie came over that evening, for Sunday dinner. She also collected the rest of her things that she had brought over. We never got one minute alone together, which was most likely for the best.

Monday morning, I officially started working with Marcus. I got to know the other men on his payroll, and a few of the women. They mostly did the office work, but there was one that got down and dirty with the rest of us. I met her on Tuesday.

"Rebecca, this is a friend of mine from the Corps, Jace. He's going to be working with us for a while." Marcus introduced me.

I shook her hand, greeting her politely. "Nice to meet you."

"Pleasure's all mine, sugar." She smiled and made a show of checking me out then smiling. Which made Marcus laugh and pat my back.

Rebecca looked to be around Angie's age, maybe a little older. She had black hair pulled into a ponytail, her eyes the color of the ocean. Her frame spoke volumes for how strong she was. In another life, I probably would have been attracted to her. The life I had before Angie.

That didn't stop her from flirting with me though. Or at least trying too.

The next Sunday, Marcus had his sister and her family over for a barbeque. Angie came too. While most of them went down to the backyard to play ball, Angie and I stayed up on the patio.

"How was your first week of school?" I asked, pretending to watch the game, but was really watching her.

Her face lit up. "It was great. The kids are adorable. And very energetic. It usually takes a couple weeks for them to settle down into a routine again, after the freedom of summer vacation."

"Did you paint your wall yet?"

"Yes. I did it on Monday, after school. It was driving me nuts. I almost did it on Sunday but wanted to make sure it had set properly first."

I held a hand over my chest. "Ouch, sweetheart. You don't trust my work?"

She shrugged. She was looking out to the field, where Kyle just got tackled by his so-called boring father. She grinned ear to ear. Whether at me or at the scene, I had no clue. I was hoping it was at me.

"How was your first week working with my dad?"

I huffed. "Good. Busy. The other workers are nice enough."

"Have you met them all yet?" She was fishing, I just wasn't sure what for.

"Yeah, I believe so. Why?"

She shrugged again. "Just curious."

Kyle dragged himself up the few steps to the raised patio and collapsed on the chair on her other side.

"Dad is a beast today."

"I see. What did you do?" She teased him.

"Nothing! I swear… at least I don't think I did."

I lifted my bottle and took a sip of the beer to cover my grin.

"What are you two talking about over here?"

"Nothing, he was telling me that he met everyone at work." Angie stated, a little too nonchalantly.

Kyle huffed in amusement, pulling himself up to grab a drink of his own from the ice chest nearby, before answering. "Oh yeah. Rebecca took quite the liking to our Major Jace over here."

Angie closed her eyes for a quick second, like she was bracing herself. "She did, huh? She's pretty."

"She's also not my type." I added, maybe a little roughly.

Kyle chuckled. "She's every man's type."

"Speaking from experience?" I asked, a quirk to my lips.

He clicked his tongue and turned his head. "Nah, she said I was too young for her. It's only five years, but whatever. You should go for it. Get out and live a little."

"He is."

My head snapped up to Marcus as he walked up with more grace than Kyle had. He reached down to the same ice chest and grabbed a bottle of water.

"Since when?" I asked, or half yelled. I saw Angie's back straighten from the corner of my eye.

"Since last night. I told her you and I would go grab drinks with her after work next Friday."

Okay, that wasn't so bad.

"She said she has a friend she wants me to meet."

Never mind, it was worse.

"Are you going on a date, daddy?" Angie snapped out of whatever funk she had slid into, focusing on her dad getting out. Just like she wanted.

Marcus grimaced. "Sort of, I guess. I'm only going to help my friend out. In the meantime, making new friends wouldn't kill me." He chugged the water quickly, clearly uncomfortable, and went back to their game.

"Speaking of getting out. Angie?"

"No." She snapped at Kyle. He laughed it off.

"Come on. You owe me one."

Angie rolled her eyes. "What, Kyle?"

Kyle jumped up, excited. "Ben is in town this weekend."

There was no mistaking her dislike for that. "Seriously?"

"Come on, please? He did me a favor a while back, and now I owe him one. You know he's always had the hots for you."

Angie let out a pathetic sounding whimper.

"Come on, cousin. Even your dad and this hermit are going out." He threw a thumb over at me. Something about that reminder sealed the deal for her.

"Fine." She growled. "But if he gets creepy again, I make no promises that his balls will survive the night."

"Done. He promised to be on his best behavior."

Angie didn't seem sold on it, but he ran off anyway.

"You don't have to go out with him."

"Yeah." She snarled at me. "And you don't have to go out with Rebecca." She stood up and walked back in the house.

I stood up to follow but Kent came running up next. "Hey, come play. We need to even out. Missy has to head off to work."

I looked to the house, sighed, then followed him to the field. Hopefully, I would be able talk to her later.

I wasn't. Nor did we see Angie for the rest of the week. I tried to message her, but she never responded. She only had to say the word and I would cancel the double date. She was the one who kept insisting that we needed distance. Not me. I'd much rather be with Angie than anyone else. Ever. But since she refused to talk to me about it, I was left with no choice but to go out with Marcus and Rebecca.

We met up at some bar across town, I hadn't paid much attention on the way there. Rebecca's friend was a redhead, and a little on the shy side. And younger than her. If I had had any hope of Marcus getting something out of tonight, that killed it. Stacey was the same age as Angie. He would never date someone that much younger.

Rebecca glued herself to my hip the second we showed up and stayed there. We walked to a restaurant close by, a Puerto Rican place. Rebecca sat next to me, forcing Marcus to sit next to Stacey. I wasn't sure who was going to owe who when this was over.

Rebecca kept my arm locked tightly in her arm until our food came. As soon as we were done, it went right back. We walked them back to the bar to have a few drinks. I only had one scotch, not wanting to give her any more ideas then she already had.

Somehow I got roped into dancing with her. When she tried to kiss me, I had had enough.

"What's wrong?" How did she have no clue?

"I'm not looking for a relationship right now." I told her, as gently as I could.

She pulled herself up against me, trying to be seductive I guess. "Neither am I. I'm just looking for some fun."

I put my hands on her forearms and pushed her back as carefully as I could. "I'm not looking for that either. I am just trying to adjust back to civilian life again."

She huffed and crossed her arms. "Seriously? You're going to go with that line?"

I laughed sardonically and rubbed my hand over my mouth. "It's not a line. It's the truth. Look, you are a very attractive woman, but I'm not looking for anything right now. A one-night stand has never been my MO. And, no offense, but you're not my type."

She huffed. "Then what is your type?"

"Softer, calmer, a little on the shy side. Doesn't know just how beautiful she really is."

Rebecca's face softened. "You already have someone in mind."

What the hell. "Yes. But she isn't in the same place yet."

"Awe, honey." She patted my shoulder. "She'll get there. Just be patient."

My head dropped. "I'm trying, Rebecca. I really am. Do you mind keeping this between us though, please?"

"Oh sure, honey. Mum's the word." She imitated zipping her lips. "Care to dance? I'll play nice this time?"

I laughed and danced with her again, this time as friends. Just friends. It only made it slightly better.

CHAPTER 11-

Angie

"What the hell was I thinking?" I shouted at the mirror, where I was trying to put mascara on.

"You were thinking… he's going out with someone, why shouldn't I?" Whit responded.

"Darn right!" Laura added. I had them all on a group video call.

"Alexander copying words again?" Nat asked.

Laura rolled her eyes. "Yes. It's annoying. All my favorite words in the English language are off limits."

"Ah, the joys of freedom. I can say what I want. Go out when I want. And screw whoever I want." Nat stated with an air of being holier than us.

"You can't hear me, but I'm cursing you out with every word I know, in my head." Laura pouted.

"Maybe this is a good thing for you. You need to expand your vocabulary." That earned me a stuck-out tongue.

"Or at least learn a new language." Whit added with a shrug. "That's what we did. Allen and I know enough Italian to speak dirty to each other and curse. The kid has no clue what we are saying. And, if she repeats it, who will understand her?"

"Ooo, there's an idea. I hadn't thought of that." Laura started clicking away on her phone, which was why we made her do these calls with a computer now. She'd forgotten about us before. A few times actually.

"Back to the topic at hand. Why did you agree to go out with creepy Ben?" Nat made a stink face. She'd met him a few years ago and had the same opinion as me about him.

I turned my phone and sank onto the toilet, only to sit. Anything else would be gross.

"Kyle owed him a favor, I owed Kyle a favor, and Ben is coming to town."

"And Jason was supposed to be going on some date with a hot construction chick." Whit threw in.

"I still can't believe we didn't even know there was a Jason until today." Laura whined, her attention still on her phone. I forgot how whiny she got when she was pregnant.

"I'm sorry, okay. It all happened fast. Then my roof caved in, school started, and oh, the guy I really, really, like happens to be my dad's best friend. Nothing going on over here."

"Why do you owe Kyle a favor? Doesn't he owe you like 50?" Nat wouldn't admit it, but she still had a thing for my cousin. They spent some time together when she interned with my dad after college. She refused to stay in Florida though, and he had no interest in leaving. I secretly believed that was why none of her relationships ever worked out. They weren't Kyle.

"Him and Jason basically rebuilt the entire ceiling over my living room. For free. It should have cost me like, thousands of dollars in labor alone. They did me a huge favor."

"And how did you repay Jason?" Whit asked.

I closed one eye and turned away, pretending to put my shoes on. The blush gave me away though, they were all cackling.

"He started it. I was tired and collapsed onto my bed. He started massaging my legs… then back… then shoulders… then… you know."

"The rub manipulation. Works every time." Whit sighed and looked at the sky like she was remembering the good times.

"You and Allen need to go on a date and get busy." Laura threw in.

"We get busy all the time, that's not the problem."

"It is if it's all about the work and not the fun. You are trying too hard to have another baby and you're stressing your body out. Go out somewhere romantic, just be together. Not for the sake of creating another offspring, but just to revel in your love."

"Wise words coming from a woman who isn't allowed to speak comfortably in her own home." Nat threw out with snark.

"Yeah, but she's right. Lately we only make love to try and get pregnant. I'm tired of it." Whit gasped dramatically. "I can't believe it. I never thought it would happen to me. I'm tired of sex."

Laura turned away from her phone and pointed at her knowingly. "That's because you made it work. You took the fun and the feelings out of it."

"How awful. I can't imagine something like that." Nat recoiled.

"I can." I snorted. Their eyes locked on mine through the screen. "Oh no. Not with Jason, that is *never* boring. But you all remember Mike, right?" They nodded. "So, boring. Off the charts, boring. I faked it more often than not."

They all grimaced. Mike was not a good time in my life. He was a rebound after a false restart with an ex. Desperate girls made desperate mistakes.

My doorbell rang and I flinched. "How do I look?"

"You failed. You still look gorgeous." Nat deadpanned.

It worked. I finally laughed. I told them all goodnight then opened the door.

I forced a smile. "Ben. How nice to see you again." Not.

Ben stepped inside, leaning in to kiss my cheek. "Angie, wow. You look great." His baby blues roamed my body a couple times. I had chosen a pair of slacks and a loose blouse. Apparently it still showed too much.

Ben wasn't bad looking. On the contrary, he was roughly 5'10, an inch or two taller than me. He had black hair and brown eyes. He was a mechanic by trade, and looked like he spent his days carrying engines around. He also had that perfect perma-tan shade going for him.

It was the way he licked his lips and made that yum sound when he checked me out that killed it for me. It was just plain creepy.

"Thanks for agreeing to come tonight. I know I've come off a little creepy in the past, and I'm hoping to make up for it."

Ya huh, so far, no change. I pulled my door closed and locked the deadbolt with my key. "Where are we going exactly?"

"Oh, I have a family thing I have to go to tonight and I didn't want to go alone."

I stopped halfway down the porch. "Family?" I dropped my shoulders. "Why? What did you tell them?"

"Nothing, really. Just that I had a girl I liked and was bringing her tonight."

I pinched the bridge of my nose. "What kind of family thing is this?"

"My grandfather's 80th birthday party." My jaw dropped and he rushed to make it all sound better. "I know it's not ideal, but I need to show him that I am maturing, growing up."

"Oh. My. Gosh. You're using me to get an inheritance!" I didn't need to ask. I already knew that he came from money. He worked because he wanted to, not because he had to. Which I always liked. Again, it was his creepy personality that was the turn off.

Ben lifted his thumb and forefinger. "Maybe a little. Come on, Kyle said you would be cool with this."

"Kyle knew about this?" I asked slowly, a growl on my lips. I was going to kill him.

"Uh, yeah. It was his idea in the first place."

"Oh, I am so going to kill him. He said he owed *you* a favor." I may have stomped my foot at the end.

Ben didn't seem fazed enough in my opinion. "Nope. I will owe him big after this though."

"Oh, no. You will owe me. Not him. Understood?" I pointed at myself, making sure he understood who I was talking about.

"Does that mean you will still come?"

I smirked. He looked like a puppy wagging his tail. "Fine. But if you cross any lines tonight. I will knee you in the balls, in front of your grandfather, and then tell him what you are doing."

He grabbed his manhood - finally reacting properly - cupping it and turning away from me. "Please don't. One more hit from you and I'm likely never to have kids."

The laugh bubbled out of me. "Flattery will get you everywhere, Mr. Garcia. Alright. Let's get this over with."

He drove us to the party in an old Mustang. Throughout the entire drive, he told me all about how he fixed it up himself. We drove to an older part of town, a neighborhood I recognized as where most of the Cubans in town lived.

Ben opened my door like a gentleman, and escorted me to the front door, his hand on my back. I had to remind myself that I was playing a part tonight - before I caved and kneed him in the balls.

I blinked my eyes at all the people inside. There had to be at least a hundred. I didn't know how they all had fit inside. It reminded me of one of those cars at the circus, where clown after clown after clown kept climbing out.

An hour in, I started recognizing people. Even worse, they recognized me.

I yanked Ben's arm until he put his ear near my very angry lips. "Why are there members of *my* family here?"

Ben looked in the direction I was looking, with my completely fake smile. "You mean the Perez familia?" He seemed surprised by that.

"Yes, Ben. That is my mother's sister, Alicia, and my grandmother Benita."

He cursed, then smiled, speaking through his own fake grin. "They are old friends of the family. I swear I didn't know. I never would have agreed to this if that were the case."

Lovely. We straightened up in time for Alicia to make it to me.

"Angela, darling! It has been too long since we've seen you." She kissed both my cheeks, then cupped them. "You have grown up. You still look so much like your papa, but I do see your mother in you. The cheekbones, and nose mostly. Just like her though, you have a simplistic beauty."

In other words, plain. I got that a lot from them. I loved my Cuban family, but they weren't thrilled that I looked so much like my dad. They used to say he muddied the pool. Mom was gorgeous. Dad was handsome. But yeah, smooth sand and clear waters still made mud. That was me.

Mud was fun to play with for a time, but no one ever kept it as a keepsake. People collected sand in jars. They might take a small capsule of water or what not. But they did not keep mud. Which pretty much summed up my life.

"What have you been doing?"

"I'm still teaching here in Miami." Not that they got in touch with me very often. To be fair, I didn't exactly call them all that often either. Again, I look more like my dad than my mom. I didn't exactly fit in with that side of my family.

Alicia's eyes traveled over to Ben and lit up. "Benny, is Angela the girl you have been speaking to everyone about?"

Oh, boy. Why did that sound like he down played everything to me?

He cleared his throat and pulled on his collar. He also very subtly turned his front away from me. Smart move. My looks may be simple, but my brain was not. Ben knew I caught what that meant.

"Yes. We didn't realize the close family connections until recently." He could say that again.

Alicia clapped, drawing more eyes our way. "That's wonderful. Papa and Alvaro immigrated together from Cuba. What a wonderful way to finally bring our families together! They wanted to in the past of course, but that's the problem with only having daughters." She squealed as she spun, grabbed both our hands, and pulled us to another room.

"You owe me sooo big for this." I hissed at him.

"You? When this all blows up, I'm dead! I was going to use the money to open my own shop."

"Oh, you poor, poor, baby. You might just have to take out a loan like the rest of us. I can't *believe* we are doing this."

We came to a stop in front of an old-fashioned, throwback to the 80's, puke ugly armchair. Ben's arm swiftly went around my waist and we both pasted on the fake smiles.

"Grandpapa, I'd like you to meet…"

"Angela!" Alicia cut Ben off, too excited to wait. "She is my niece."

Glad to know they approved of this relationship. Wonder what they would say if they found out that I really wanted another Gringo. One closer to my dad's age than mine.

"Oh, so you are Marta's daughter." He studied me, a slight frown on his face. "You don't look much like her."

"No, I look more like my father." I added, carefully. Maybe I would get lucky, and he would disapprove of me. The older generations had more issues with mixed marriages.

"You have her mannerisms though. It helps one to see the similarities more." Shucks. So close. "So, you are the one my grandson has been hiding."

"Apparently so." It was hard work keeping the fake smile up. To help, I imagined how satisfying it was going to be when I kicked Ben's balls in later.

Alvaro thought this was quite funny for some reason. "How come I haven't met you sooner? Your family is here all the time."

"My father was a Marine, we traveled with him as often as we could. After mama died, he left and brought me home, so we could be near family. Not long after, I went off to college and started teaching."

"Teaching. A good career. I was sorry to hear about your mother. She was as sweet as can be."

I only nodded. I didn't like talking about my mom. Especially to people that knew her. They always wanted to relive this memory of her or that memory. While it wasn't necessarily a bad thing, my most prominent memory of her was that last day. Watching her struggle to breathe.

"Ah, my apologies. I'm sure it is not easy speaking about your mother, even after all these years. We learn to keep moving along, but we never truly get over the loss of a loved one."

Hallelujah! I smiled, for real this time. "Thank you. Yes, it can be hard. But I do love to think of her."

He nodded and turned to Ben. "I wasn't sure I believed you when you said you were finally starting to settle down. And with a Perez! This calls for a toast!"

Settling down?? What the hell did he tell them?

To my utter horror, he announced our *relationship* to the masses, and they all toasted and congratulated us. I was going to be committing a double homicide before the night was out.

Kyle and Ben were both dead men.

I listened as Ben spun a fairytale about us meeting through my cousin, Kyle. How we were friends for years, until one day he finally got up the courage to ask me out. He had his captive audience eating out of the palm of his hands.

He was so dead.

I suffered through the ordeal for three hours. Eating any small appetizer that came around. By the end of it, my face hurt from all the forced smiling.

"Food. Now." I commanded as soon as he started the car.

"Love too. I wish they would give out real food at these things." He turned and finally caught onto the scowl. "Oh, come on, Angie. It isn't that bad."

"Not that bad?" Seriously? Apparently he was stupider than I thought.

"You hardly see this side of the family. The next time you see them, you can just tell them that we decided we were better off as friends."

My laugh was dark and completely sarcastic.

"Please don't hit me." He moved one hand down to block his jewels just in case. I would never do it while he was driving. That would be dangerous for me too.

"I won't, but my father might. With his *shotgun*." I made sure to add a little emphasis on the last word and give him half a smirk. My daddy had a reputation. A well-earned reputation.

Ben's face paled. "Why would you tell him?!"

"I won't need to. How long do you think it will be before my Tia Alicia calls my dad and asks why he didn't tell her I was practically engaged to their family friends? This is something that should have been shared. I will not lie to my father. I do not keep secrets from him."

"Really?" He asked incredulously. "You've never kept a secret from your dad?"

Um, okay, maybe one. One big one. "No." I scoffed, trying to hide the truth.

"Kyle swears there is something going on between you and that Major working with your dad." Ben had that holier than thou, I know something, attitude.

"Wh… what? Me and Jace?"

Ben smirked. He totally knew I was lying. I wasn't actually.

"There isn't anything going on. If there was, why would I have agreed to go out with you tonight?" His smile melted and I relaxed. "Jace is my dad's best friend. I would never come between that." Also, the truth.

"Good point." We'd known each other long enough that Ben knew how much I loved my dad. "Just, please don't say anything. If he does find out, maybe ask him to keep it a secret too."

Ben pulled up to a Taco Bell and got in line.

"This pit you are digging is going to keep getting deeper and deeper. Lying is never the answer, Ben."

He sighed, finally showing some sense. "I know. But did you see how happy and proud my grandfather was tonight?"

"Ben, you work hard in that shop. You restored this car for crying out loud! That is something to be proud of. Schemes like this hide that though."

"He, uh, he doesn't know about the shop."

I spun in my seat. "What?"

"I haven't told any of them. They only know that I dropped out of law school."

I rubbed my forehead as he pulled up to the speaker to order. We took our food to a park nearby and sat at one of the picnic tables.

"Why didn't you tell them about wanting to own your own shop?"

He shrugged. "I don't know. They were all so happy when I got into law school, I thought they would be disappointed."

"They are going to be more disappointed that you lied to them, then they will be about your career choices. You need to come clean, soon. Before this all blows up in your face."

"I know." Well, now instead of looking like a puppy, he looked like I kicked his puppy.

I let him kiss my cheek when he dropped me off, then collapsed on my bed and laughed maniacally at the ridiculous night I had. It was better than crying. Something I had *not* been doing every night for the last two weeks, in the dark of the night, when I'd subconsciously reach over and find an empty pillow next to me.

Nope. Never happened.

CHAPTER 12

Jason

Saturday was quiet. Marcus and I played some cards together, again, and watched a movie, again. Sunday followed the same pattern.

"I can see why you went to such lengths to get us out of the house more." I lifted my beer to my lips then paused and looked at the bottle. "Do you think I am becoming an alcoholic? I think I've drank more in the last few weeks than I did all last year."

Marcus lifted his feet onto the coffee table, his arms folded across his chest, his eyes focused on the Marvel marathon we had going. I had missed most of them, being stationed in third world countries could do that to you.

"No. You rarely have more than 2 a day. And going out blew up in our faces in a pretty big way."

I snorted. "You can say that again. I've never felt so pathetic in my life."

His head rolled along the back of the couch to look at me. "What happened with that friend you made at the airport?"

Now I remembered why I was drinking so much more than usual. "There were complications we didn't expect."

"What does that mean? Didn't you like her?"

"A lot. Still do. We've spoken a few times, but… I don't know. I guess it's just not the right timing. Like I said, unforeseen complications."

"Can't you give me a little bit more to go on?" I laughed as his voice went up a few octaves on little.

I shrugged, trying to make it sound like it wasn't a big deal. "Just some drama with her family. There is a lot of baggage there. I don't really want to get into it."

He turned back to the movie. "You'd be surprised how many complications are just an ant hill turned into a molehill. I'm willing to bet the family complications are just really you two over-thinking things."

I snorted. "Doubt it. For one, there is a tad bit of an age difference."

He made a phfftt sound and waved it off. "That's not an issue. As soon as Angela started dating, I told her she could date anyone older than her but younger than me."

I choked as the sudden laugh came out of me. That was good to know. And explained a whole hell of a lot. No wonder she hardly blinked an eye when I told her.

"Why older than her?"

"Because women mature faster than men. And she has always been more mature than most girls her age. The boys? Forget about it."

"That's true."

"Hit me with the next one, let's solve all these and get you a life."

I chuckled. "Can't talk about the next ones. Her personal business, sorry."

He flipped me off and I laughed. I wished I could tell him. But there was a chance that she was right, and he would get upset. I still needed him. And so did she. I certainly still needed any inch that she was willing to give me. Which would all be gone if I told him without talking to her first.

We got through most of the movie *Thor* before his phone rang. He rolled his eyes and paused the movie.

"Hello, Alicia… Yes, I know it's been a while."

He looked at me and made a gesture to kill him now. I had to laugh. Was he demonstrating how little we boys ever grew up, or how little he wanted to speak to the woman? I stopped laughing when his feet hit the floor with a resounding thunk, and he sat up straight.

It seemed serendipitous that Angie walked in right then. Marcus' eyes automatically glued to her, a look that showed extreme disapproval. He curled his finger, telling her to come here.

Her eyes shot to me, I shrugged. He snapped his fingers and pointed at the ground. Angie looked completely dumbfounded as to what was going on.

"No, I knew nothing about this. If I had, I would have told you, Alicia. Months, you say?"

Angie grimaced and slowly started walking backward. I leaned back, beginning to enjoy this more than the movie. Marcus waved a finger side to side, telling her no. She slumped and leaned against the wall.

"Ya huh… Right. Well, she just walked in, and it sounds like we need to have a little chat… Yes, I will let you know if they set a date."

Okay, that didn't sound so funny anymore.

"Thank you, Alicia. Tell your mama hello for me… Adios." He ended the call, threw his phone on the coffee table, then leaned back, arms crossed. "Something you need to share with the class, little missy."

She swallowed, then looked at me, terrified. "It wasn't my fault. Blame it on Kyle."

"Nu huh. Try again."

"No, seriously. It's all his fault. He lied to me, saying Ben asked for a favor. A simple date. I owed him for the whole roof thing, so I agreed. Turns out, Kyle was the one who told Ben to take me to this family party thing last night. He was trying to prove to his grandfather that he was maturing."

I choked on the laugh, earning a scowl from Marcus. Which made the laugh slip out. He knew why I was laughing, and his face slipped as well. I mean, the timing of the example and his words just moments ago… it was funny. And the whole thing was utterly ridiculous.

Angie was on a roll though and kept going. "I went under protest. I told him it was ridiculous. He swore it was a one-time thing. Neither of us had any idea that his grandfather and my abuelo were old friends. As soon as Alicia saw me the whole thing got blown out of portion. Ben spun all these stories making it sound like we'd been together for months and things were serious." Her eyes were pleading with me. "I swear, I haven't seen him in years. I can't even stand the little bugger."

I nodded. I got it. She was schemed against as much as the rest of them. She turned back to her dad, who looked like he was ready to kill someone.

Angie swore and kicked the floor. "I told Ben they were going to call you. I just thought I had more time. Ben said if they did, to beg you to not say anything."

"We do not lie in this house or keep secrets, young lady."

I felt that barb as much as she did. "I know, daddy. I was going to tell you anyway. I don't know what to do here. Abuelo Alvaro was so happy, and it was his 80th birthday. I didn't want to ruin that for him. We were already there when everything went down. I couldn't do that to him or mama's familia."

Marcus lifted his arm, and she came and curled between us on the couch. He held her the same way I saw him do a hundred times when she was little, even kissing her forehead.

"How do you manage to get in these pickles?"

"How the hell should I know? I didn't even want to go out with him last night." She pouted, and it was kind of cute. I wanted to bite that plump lip she had sticking out.

"Next time, follow those instincts."

Angie laughed, kissed his cheek, then sat up. Her fingers brushed against mine, the craving to touch her intensified.

"How did your night on the town go?" Her head swiveled back and forth. We both grimaced, she laughed. "Come on, it couldn't have been that bad?" Her head settled on me. "Did you not like Rebecca?"

I huffed. "Not my type. I said that before."

"She was all for it though." Marcus chuckled. "She held onto him like she was afraid he would run away, and then was practically all over him on the dance floor."

I knew Angie well enough that I could tell her smile wasn't real. "I thought men liked that?"

"Not all men." I told her. I had a lot more I wanted to say, but I couldn't in front of her dad. Especially not after the whole we don't lie and keep secrets, bit. "The friend she brought for your dad was cute though."

Her grin grew, for real this time, as she turned back to him. "Yeah?"

"No." He said flatly. "You don't date anyone older than me, and I won't date anyone younger than you."

She moved her head side to side, thinking about it. "Yeah, I'm good with that."

He sighed out a "thank you" as he stood up. "Now I need a beer."

"I swear, nothing happened with her." I whispered to her.

Angie smiled. "I know. And nothing happened with Ben." That stupid sad face was back. I wanted to kiss it, but the Cap was back already. "What are you guys watching?"

And just like that, she joined us in our pathetic marathon. Although, just her there added a little more life to the room. She also added chips and dip. Then made us dinner. She laughed at some of the stupidest parts, which made us laugh.

It was official. I was in trouble. No one would ever compare to Angela Carson in my book. Now I just had to figure out how to convince her of that.

The next day, Marcus told the boys to meet us at their parents' place. The second they got out of the truck, he cornered Kyle. It wasn't hard, seeing as the boy took one look at his face and tried to run. Kent and I had a good laugh.

"I swear, Uncle Marcus, I didn't know it would be that bad!" His arms were waving in front of him, crossing each other.

"The family connections shouldn't have mattered. How dare you put your cousin in that position!"

Kyle squeaked and flinched at the tenor of Marcus' voice. Kent and I nearly fell over laughing. He was even wiping a tear from under his eye.

"This has always been one of my favorite pastimes, watching him get railed by the parentals."

"I take it that this is a common occurrence."

"Not so much in recent years, but when we were younger, oh yeah. Sweet little Angela never had an issue tattling on him. He got away with so much more before they came home for good. And yet, he still loves her."

"That may be why he roped her into this. Payback."

Kent thought about that for a second. "You know, I think you're right. Watch this. Hey, Uncle Marcus?"

Marcus turned, his smile showing for the first time. He was enjoying the moment too.

"Think maybe Kyle put Angie in that position as payback for all the times he's gotten in trouble because of her?"

Kyle's middle finger went up fast but was too slow going back down. Marcus caught it in his fist and turned it until Kyle was repeatedly saying ow and practically on his knees.

"Let's see what your mother has to say about this." Marcus started dragging him, by the middle finger, toward the front door.

"Please, don't. Please, Uncle Marcus? I'll work overtime for a month, for free! Just please don't rat me out to my mother."

"Rat you out for what? What did you do now?" Too late. Kathy had heard the commotion and came outside, hands on her hips.

Kyle looked like he was about to pee his pants.

By the time they came back to us, Kyle looked like a properly scolded child. Holding his finger like it was broken against his chest. Kent and I laughed harder. Marcus was sporting a pretty big grin as well. I patted Kyle on the back as he walked around to load into my truck. He and I had a roof we were working on with two other men. Marcus and Kyle were meeting their team for an extension on a house they'd been working on.

"Guess I should be glad it was Uncle Marcus and not Angie." He mumbled as soon as we were on the road.

I laughed. "Why is that?"

"Because she bites and hits low. Ben said he was on guard all night on Saturday. At least until they left the party. I guess things went better after that."

"I thought she didn't like him?"

Kyle shrugged and shook out his finger. "I don't know. He can be full of it at times, but he's always had a thing for her. It's why I suggested he take her. See if it would help any. She's all heart that cousin of mine. And Ben is a bit pathetic when it comes to dealing with his family."

"What do you mean?" My grip tightened on the steering wheel.

Kyle leaned back, relaxing more the further away we got from Marcus and Kathy. "Well, have you noticed how Ang doesn't quite realize how pretty she is? She thinks less of herself?"

"Yeah."

"That's kind of the way Ben is when it comes to his family. He is afraid of disappointing them, so he lies about things." He looped his hand around in a wave. "Like the party thing. Ben graduated top of his class both in high school and with his undergrad in communications. He even got into Harvard Law. They were thrilled. And then disappointed and confused when he dropped out three months in. As far as they know, he is on the beach or some friend's yacht every day."

"Where is he really?"

"Underneath cars and covered in motor oil. He works in an auto shop in the Keys. His grandfather is loaded and is supposed to give him an inheritance when he dies. Ben is freaked out because they think he is lazy and irresponsible. He wants to use the money to open a shop of his own one day. So, we thought, if he took Angie, who is the embodiment of responsibility, it would show them he isn't what they think. Worked out better than we planned to. The families are close, they are very excited about the prospect of joining the two families."

I had to remind myself to keep my breathing steady and to focus on driving.

"Ben said they had a nice night after. A quick dinner and just chatting. She usually doesn't give him the time of day. She took pity on him after she heard his story."

"So, you *are* trying to set her up with your friend?"

"Maybe, I don't know. She'd be good for him though. Hey, you missed our turn. You all right?"

"Huh? Oh yeah, just still getting the hang of how the streets work here."

Kyle didn't question it, just pointed out the directions. I let him, as my mind was too far gone. I knew the time when someone else would come knocking on her door would come eventually. I just thought I had more time.

CHAPTER 13

Angie

"Miss Carson?" I looked up from my desk, where I was eating my lunch, and saw the school principal, Mrs. Tucker, peeking her head around the corner. She was a tough old broad and reminded me of my dad in some ways. If she wasn't happily married, I'd try and set them up.

"Yes?"

"You have a delivery in the office. I told Linda I would let you know as I passed by." She looked amused and curious but didn't say anything else.

Curious myself, I stood up, closing my leftover lasagna from dinner at dad's last night. "What is it?"

"A surprise." She winked at me then walked away.

Confused, I turned the opposite direction she went and walked down the hall toward the front office. As soon as I pushed through the door, I gasped. What the hell?

"Please tell me, those are *not* for me."

Linda laughed and waved to them. "They most certainly are. I didn't know you were dating anyone."

"I'm not." I reached in and pulled the small card out.

Again, I am so, so sorry about the other night. I will make it up to you, I promise.

Dinner on the beach? I hear you like Cuban, which totally makes sense now.

Call me, Ben

At the bottom was a phone number, I assumed his.

"Well, who's it from?" Mrs. Tucker asked, walking back into the office. I was pretty sure she faked running an errand.

"Um, a friend of my cousin. He's apologizing for a misunderstanding over the weekend."

"Ooh, this is a good apology. They are beautiful."

They were at that. I wondered if Kyle told him Tulips were my favorite. These were a mix of white and purple ones. I leaned in and smelled them, before saying goodbye and taking them to my classroom.

I stared at them for a few minutes before deciding to message him.

Me: The flowers were unnecessary. But thank you.

I opened my lunch back up and finished the last few bites before his response came.

Ben: Yes, they were. I owe you big time and I feel awful. I feel like I am always making mistakes when it comes to you. Let me make it up to you? Please?

I tapped my phone on my leg, trying to decide what to do. I didn't want to date Ben. But did that mean we couldn't be friends?

Certain other people might take it the wrong way though. I didn't know why it mattered. We weren't together and we most likely never would be. As much as that pained me to say, or even think.

Ben: Please? *puppy begging GIF*

I laughed. I wondered how many people told him he looked like a puppy?

Me: Fine, Friday, but only as friends. This is NOT a date.
Ben: Not a date, got it. Just two friends. I promise to TRY and remember that.

I smirked. He was incorrigible.

The bell rang, and I quickly put my lunch supplies away. By the time I got outside, the kids were all lined up and ready for me. Lindsay was our line leader today, so I waved for her to take them all inside. Where we then dug into some bowls of dirt so we could play archaeologist and look for fossils.

Friday evening, I changed into a pair of jeans and a nicer version of a t-shirt, the front tucked in with the back loose. I had on a pair of heels, ones that would be easy to take off so we could walk in the sand. He did say we could eat on the beach. A little romantic for two people who are just friends, but I liked the beach.

Ben greeted me with a kiss on the cheek and did not lick his lips as he checked me out this time.

"Wow. You look great. Change your mind on this being a date?" He gave me that cocky half grin.

"Not a chance."

He snapped his fingers in a shucks motion, and I laughed. We ate at a cute little mom and pop Cuban place I hadn't been to before. They even had a patio overlooking the beach. After dinner, we walked in the sand, and just talked about random things. It was nice.

"Thank you for dinner." I told him, as he walked me to my door.

"Thank you for letting me make it up to you. I really am sorry all that got so out of hand."

"Oh, I know. I told you my dad already knows. It's going to come back to bite you in the butt soon."

He frowned and nodded. "Yeah, I know."

I put a hand on his shoulder and playfully pushed him back. "Ben, man up and talk to your family. That will make the most difference."

He rubbed a hand through his hair and gave an aggrieved sigh. "Growing up sucks."

"Yes, it does. But it does come with perks."

"True. Can I kiss you?"

Uh, say what now? I pressed my lips together, trying to find a nice way to put this.

"Still, no, huh?"

I laughed and shook my head. "No. I'm sorry. I misjudged you in the beginning, you are sweeter than the way you come off at first, but no. You're just not my type."

"I'm thinking your type is a bit older, and military."

"Ben…"

"Nah, it's all good. I get it. I won't tell anybody, honest. Not even Kyle."

I tried to play it off by rolling my eyes, but his chuckle said he wasn't buying it. He put a hand out to me for a shake.

"Friends?"

I put my hand in his and shook it. "Friends."

I went inside and closed the door, still laughing softly.

I woke up the next morning excited for the weekend. I took care of a few errands, and things that needed to be done around the house. Like laundry and dishes that had piled up. I tried to finish anything I would need to so I wouldn't have to do anything else over the weekend.

Sunday morning, I went over a little earlier than I normally would, a bag packed. I planned to stay the night, since there was no school on Monday for Labor Day. We always had a big family barbeque on holidays.

I walked in just after lunch, bag in hand.

"Hey, buttercup. You're early!" Dad walked over to me, greeting me with a big hug. "You staying the night, too?"

"Yeah, if you don't mind. Since tomorrow is Labor Day, I didn't see any sense in driving home."

"I don't mind at all, you know that. Oh," he turned, pulling me further into the living room. "You remember Rebecca, don't you?"

Of course, I did. She was a knockout and built things. "Yes, of course. Hi. How are you?" I reached over to where she sat next to

Jason on the couch and shook her hand. Which was somewhat entangled with his arm.

"Well, hey there. Haven't seen you in a while."

"Nope, what's going on? I'm not interrupting anything am I?"

"No." Jason stood up abruptly and walked around to pick up my bag. "We're all just hanging out. I'll take this to your room."

"Sure, thank you." I would have followed him, but I had no reason to, and there were too many eyes on me. It was probably for the best. We didn't exactly have a good record with being alone. And I wasn't sure I wanted the answers to the questions rolling around inside my head.

"This is my friend, Shelly." Rebecca pointed to another woman.

I expected to see someone younger, with red hair. Instead, this one was older, with blonde hair and subtle strips of gray. Or was it white? Rebecca must have found an older friend to bring along this time.

I waved at her, not moving from where I stood. "Nice to meet you."

She returned the sentiment, her eyes glancing to my dad. Who still stood next to me, his arm around my waist like I was his lifeline.

"I didn't know you were planning to have company today. I would have come later."

"Nonsense." He said, pulling me toward the love seat that sat against the wall. He sat with me. Apparently I was his shield as well as his lifeline. "You are always welcome to come over."

"We stopped by and thought we would surprise the men, see if they wanted to go to a movie with us." Rebecca graciously gave me the context I was missing.

"Oh, how lovely." Not.

"It's wonderful that you come to visit your dad. My son moved up North and doesn't get down as often as I would like. Where do you live?" Shelly asked me.

"Um, here in Miami. We have family dinner every weekend."

"Your daddy must have raised you right. It's nice to see such a bond."

"Nah, it was more her mother. I just tagged along for the ride." He quipped with his usual response.

Jason came down a minute later, the tension still just as thick. He looked around the room, obviously not sure where to sit. He settled for leaning against the wall.

Rebecca scooted over on the couch an inch, patting the seat next to her. "Why don't you come sit back down, love?"

My eyes widened at the nickname and looked at Jason. He looked slightly irritated. Did he mean what he said about her not being his type? Or was he just trying to find a way to let me down easy that he had already moved on?

"I'm good here, thanks. Need to stretch out the old legs."

Rebecca giggled, sounding like a teenager. "Silly, you're not that old." She stood and walked over to him, wrapping her claws around his arm again. He patted them somewhat absently.
And that was enough for me.

"You know what?" I stood up. "I forgot I promised to call someone back this afternoon. I'm just going to head on up to my room and give you all some privacy."

"Who did you forget to call? Whit? Nat?" My dad asked, his eyes practically begging me to stay.

I couldn't though. I couldn't sit there and watch Jason with a woman who was twice as pretty as me and slightly closer to his age. A decade was better than a decade and a half.

My eyes went right to Jason's as I answered. "Ben."

"I thought you two weren't getting along?"

I looked back to my dad to answer. I didn't want to see the pain in Jason's eyes again. I wanted to be mad at him, not feel guilty for hurting him. I had no excuse for either. We weren't together. He was free to date whoever he wanted. Just as I was. His side had obviously faded already, why hadn't mine?

"He apologized and has been trying to make it up to me. He's not as bad as I thought he was, to be honest." My dad looked confused but nodded. I kissed his cheek. "I'll be upstairs if you need me." I refused to make eye contact with Jason as I left the room.

"Well, she seems sweet." Shelly sounded like she was trying to break an awkward silence.

I didn't care if I left it awkward in there. It shouldn't matter to me.

I had to force myself not to slam my door like a child having a temper tantrum. I still sank to the floor and started crying though. Eventually I moved to my bed, my knees to my chest, my face buried between them.

Twenty minutes later, I heard the front door open and close a few times. Followed by a knock on my door. I didn't say anything. I hoped he would get the point and go away.

He didn't. And apparently I hadn't locked the door either.

Too soon, a pair of arms I knew better than I should, wrapped around me.

"It wasn't what it looked like. I swear."

"Tell that to the woman who was glued to your hip. *Love.*"

Jason huffed at my emphasis. "I did, multiple times. And she still keeps coming back." He rubbed my arms and kissed my head. "Ben?"

I snorted. "Just friends. He may not be the cretin I once thought he was, but he still has a lot of growing up to do before I would give him the time of day."

"Hmm. So, you're still single, and I'm still single…" He bent his head down and started kissing the bare part of my shoulders. I should have worn sleeves.

I sniffed and pushed away from him, off the bed. "And you're still my dad's best friend."

Jason groaned and fell onto his back.

"How has your thigh been doing?"

"Fine. I've been running in the mornings lately. It helps stretch the muscle out after sleeping. I had a better way to exercise it, but *someone* cut me off." He sat back up and winked at me.

"I'm glad it's doing better. Did your dates leave?"

"Criminy." He stood up and stalked toward me, backing me against the wall since I was trying to get away from him. "They showed up out of the blue. I thought Rebecca and I had reached an understanding last week. I thought wrong. And yes, they are gone. Your dad went to pick up Chinese for dinner."

"Beef and broccoli? Egg rolls?" I brought my head up to look at him and he laughed.

"Yes, he seems to be under the impression that it was all too weird for you and now he has to suck up. I was tempted to tell him it was my fault, but I thought that would put me further into the dog house." Jason lifted my hand and kissed my knuckles, his eyes on mine. "I've missed you."

I snorted. "Right because we saw each other so much before a few weeks ago."

He grazed his other hand down the side of my face and my eyes closed. "Doesn't change the fact that I missed you. I've tried to message you, call you, but you don't answer." His voice was as soft as his touch. He was trying to hypnotize me. And it was working. How did he gain so much power over me so quickly?

"I never know what to say." He hummed and started kissing around my jaw. "You're not playing fair." I accused him.

He chuckled and kept going. "I don't care. I finally have you in my grasp again. I told you before, I can't resist not touching you. Every Sunday evening is pure torture. You sit right next to me on the couch, and I can't so much as touch your hand." He took both of them in his hands and held them over my head. He braced them there with one of his large ones, while the other gripped my waist.

Jason started leaving soft kisses all over my face, but never on my lips.

"Is this payback, then? Torture for torture?"

He laughed softly but didn't stop. "Am I torturing you?"

"Yes, and you know it. Sitting next to you isn't exactly easy for me either, you know."

"Hmm, I'm glad to hear it. It's hard to tell when you won't talk to me. I enjoy talking to you."

I whimpered as his hand slid up my side, pushing the tank top up with it. His lips finally came close enough that I was able to lean forward and catch them. He growled, suddenly done with his game and dropped my hands. They found their home behind his head and around his neck. He lifted my leg, and I wrapped it around him.

We fell into an easy rhythm. Inside our own little bubble. He had my shirt to my neck, ready to rip it off, when my phone dinged in my pocket. We ignored it. Until it dinged again. He reached into the back pocket of my jean shorts and pulled it out. He glanced at it, froze, then stepped back, away from me. He handed me my phone like it was contaminated with COVID.

"What?" I took it and saw the first line of the most recent message sitting on the lock screen.

Ben: Thanks again for last night…

I cursed and put my finger on the back to unlock my phone with my fingerprint.

"I thought it might be your dad." Jason stuttered, rubbing both hands down his face. "What happened to only being friends?"

"We are." I tapped to bring up the full message. It wasn't much better.

Ben: Thanks again for last night. It was fun. Hope to do it again sometime. And don't worry, your secret is safe with me.

"Yeah, sure sounds like it."

I stepped to the side, blocking him from walking out the door. "He wanted to make up for last week, so I let him take me to dinner. *As Friends*. He knows that it will only ever be *as friends*."

Jason gave me a sarcastic laugh and shook his head. I pulled my shirt down, realizing it was still showing a bit much for this conversation.

"It doesn't matter though, does it? Wasn't that his little story to the family? You were both friends at first? No matter what I say, no matter what I do. You are still going to keep pushing me away. What will it take, Angie? I've been wracking my brain, trying to find ways to prove to you that I am all in. But I can't think of anything. I've tried everything. Just tell me, what do you want?"

"You. Okay. I want you. But you're not mine to have!"

He growled and pushed me against the door. "But I am. Just say the word and I am all yours."

I was tempted. It was right there on my lips, ready to just say "word." He could be mine. We could end this never-ending torment. I opened my lips to say it. He held his breath, moving closer, ready to pounce.

Then the front door opened.

"I'm back!"

My whole body sank into the door. Jason released the breath and set his head next to mine against the door.

"But you aren't. You are his. You have always been his. I've taken enough things away from him in my life. I can't take you too. No matter how much I want to. You don't see it. You didn't see him before you came. He is happier, lighter, freer. You are giving him his life back. I can't take that from him." I barely had the energy to whisper the words.

"And what about you? What do you get? Stolen moments when his back is turned?"

I put my hand up and rubbed his cheek. "I got a night in an airport with the most amazing man. I got a few nights of getting to feel what it was like to be with him. And I get to know that I am not hurting the man who sacrificed his dreams for me."

"Angie."

I let Jason wipe the tears from my face before I arched my back against the door enough to push me off, moving us both to stand up straight.

"Come on, or there will be no Chinese donuts left. The man has a weakness for them."

Jason picked up my hand and kissed it one more time. "I've seen him pack away two dozen in a sitting before. I *know* how he is with those."

CHAPTER 14

Jason

This woman was going to kill me. Marcus didn't want her sacrificing anything for him. But if I told him, she would be mad at me. And that was the last thing that I wanted. Seeing the anger, and hurt, in her eyes when Rebecca grabbed my arm again was bad enough.

As soon as Angie was out of the room, I had moved away and set Rebecca straight. Again. She claimed she was just trying to have a little fun. At least Shelly seemed nicer, and older. Although, she was a bit stuck on how often Angie came to visit and even stay with her dad, *and* they lived in the same city. I was pretty sure her son moved away because she was so needy.

We should have ignored Angie's phone. I was more than happy to, then I thought it might be Marcus. He would be worried if she didn't respond. There were always so many obstacles standing in our way. If I could, I would turn back time. All the way to when we were trapped in that airport together. And then I'd freeze it. Nothing had been better than our time there.

Okay, maybe the night we worked on her wall. That was a pretty good night too. Any night I had with Angie was a good night. A great night. A perfect night.

I followed her down the stairs and to the dining room. Marcus had even pulled out the glass plates, the suck up, and opened all the containers.

"Yum. Smells good." Angie sniffed the room dramatically. "Did you do something wrong?" Marcus laughed and pulled her in for a hug. She wiped a little sugar off the stubble on his jaw. "Did you at least leave any donuts for us?

He threw his head back and laughed hard, then sheepishly grabbed a half empty box off the counter.

"Here, nosey nellie. And no, I didn't do anything wrong. I just felt bad for that awkward situation you walked in on. I never should have agreed to drinks last week. It seems I've pulled the pin out of the grenade and can't fit it back in."

I pulled out a chair and sat down, snatching a donut out of the box. I set it on Angie's plate, then grabbed one of my own. "Yeah, and it keeps blowing up in my direction. Thanks for that."

Marcus sat down in the chair across from me. We had somehow created normal spots on Sundays. Marcus across from me, and Angie next to me. I wasn't going to complain, and I sure as hell wasn't going to put a spotlight on it.

"Isn't that what buddies are for? To throw themselves on a live grenade for the other?"

I picked up the beef and broccoli and poured a good size portion on Angie's plate. After that I started unloading kung pao chicken on my own. "No. We push your butt the other direction. But I will keep your version in mind the next time that grenade threatens to explode. You can take Rebecca."

Marcus grimaced. "No, thank you. If she wasn't so good at her job I'd can her."

"That's kind of sexist." Angie dumped half a box of rice onto my plate before doing her own.

"How is that sexist? I have a female working on a construction crew!" Marcus set his chopsticks down.

"So? If a man was harassing the female employees, you'd fire him. Wouldn't matter how good he was at his job. The same should be said for the women. She stopped by your house, uninvited, on a weekend. With a friend. Jace told her repeatedly that he wasn't interested, and yet, she was still rubbing up all over him." Angie shoved a bite into her mouth angrily. "If you do it to one gender, you have to do it to the other. It's only fair."

"Huh." Marcus picked up his chopsticks and continued serving up his own plate. "I didn't think of it like that. Still, I'll talk to her first, warn her of the consequences."

Marcus changed the topic and asked about school. Angie could talk for hours about her students. And we both could listen for hours. The woman had both of us wrapped around her fingers.

After dinner, we continued with our Marvel marathon. We were now up to Iron Man 3. Angie snuggled between the two of us, a blanket draped over her, her head on Marcus' shoulder, and her feet pressing against my leg. Since the blanket was there, I went ahead and placed my hand on her ankles. It was better than nothing.

The room had gone quiet around the time people started healing by fire in the movie. By the end of it, I was the last man standing. Or rather, sitting. Angie was asleep on her dad's shoulder. Marcus was asleep on his daughter's head.

Carefully, I picked Angie up and carried her up the stairs. I laid her on the bed, then carefully covered her with her comforter. Which was when she woke up, her finger grazing gently down my cheek. I kissed her softly, since this was one of those rare moments when her walls were down. She tried to turn it into more.

I pulled back with a smile. "I need to go wake your dad. He won't be happy with any of us if I leave him on that couch all night."

"Hmph. Fine." She pouted, then began squirming around under the blanket.

"What are you doing?" I was trying not to laugh, since she could be cranky when tired, and not getting lucky.

She didn't answer, but soon, she was dropping her shorts on the floor, quickly followed by her bra. Her light pink top still firmly in place.

"Much better." She sighed and snuggled down into her pillows and closed her eyes. "Have fun trying to wake him."

I caught my hand midway down to her, about faced, and practically marched out of her room. She was giggling by the time I closed her door.

Somewhat impatiently, I softly slapped Marcus' face, getting rougher as I went. I felt like dawn was going to approach by the time I even got him standing. I was pretty sure his eyes never fully opened as I herded him up the stairs and down the hall to his room. I sort of just pushed him with one finger, mentally yelling timber. He crashed on the bed, bounced once, and I left.

I stood outside her door, debating whether I should go in. We were stuck in this loop. During the day, she put distance between us, but at night…

I should just cut the cord. Hold my ground. Be firm. If we weren't going to be together, then we shouldn't be doing any of this.

I almost had myself convinced. I'd like to think I was turning away and headed for my own room. It was healthier.

But then she opened her door. And there she stood. Light pink tank, dark red underwear with pencils on them, and her hair a mess from laying in the bed. She didn't say anything. She just lifted a hand, an invitation. One I had never been able to ignore.

I stripped as I walked through her room, toward the now messed up bed. It looked like she had been tossing and turning for hours. Angie laid down in the middle, on her back. I crawled over her until my lips met hers, and her legs wrapped themselves around me.

Who was I kidding? I'd never be able to walk away from this woman.

For the first time in weeks, I slept through the night, no dreams, no nightmares. More than once over the last few months, I'd woken up in a sweat, reaching for my gun. The running wasn't just for the exercise. I woke up needing to move. Needing to do something. Running helped.

But Angie helped. Her presence soothed my soul. And when I did wake up, I got to move in a much more fun way.

I kissed her softly a few more times, not quite ready to move off her. Her hands moved up and down my arms, then my torso. I moved down her jaw… then laughed when she yawned.

"Tired already?"

"Hmm. Yes. I've been sleeping, but it doesn't seem to be enough lately."

I pushed onto my elbows, creating more space so I could see her better. "Are you getting sick?"

She shook her head with a slight frown. "I don't think so. My stomach gets a little queasy once in a while, but I think it's just stress. It has been an interesting start to the school year."

"That's true. Why don't you go back to sleep for a little bit? The others won't be here for a few more hours. Rest." I started pulling away, but she locked her ankles behind me.

"I didn't say you could leave yet." Angie started kissing my neck and rocked her hips a few times. When I still didn't cave to what she wanted, she added the nail to my coffin. "I missed you, too."

My will crumpled like a paper in flames. I gave her what she needed, and then she fell asleep. I held her for as long as I could, then collected my clothes and snuck back into my room. After a quick shower, I joined Marcus downstairs and started helping him get everything ready.

Three hours later, Angie descended, showered, and dressed in a pair of black shorts that made her butt pop and a white tank top that showed the outline of her bra. Her hair was tied in two braids, both coming over her shoulders.

Marcus hardly blinked an eye. Me on the other hand, I blinked many times and had to discreetly fix my pants. I missed my camo uniform. Those pants were baggier than my jeans.

"Morning, buttercup. You slept late."

As if on cue, Angie yawned again. My eyebrows creased.

"Yeah. Sorry. Guess I needed the day off today more than I thought. Do you need me to help with anything?"

"No. We're mostly done. Your Aunt Kathy is bringing the sides. I just need to heat the grill. Dad said he was bringing the buns. Grab a drink and take a load off." He walked forward and kissed her head. "You work too much."

Angie snorted. "Look who's talking."

Marcus grinned as he walked outside to start the grill. I took his place next to her.

"Are you sure you're okay?"

She lifted a hand and patted my chest, like she was comforting me. "I'm fine. Really. I just need to move around some." I lifted my eyebrows suggestively and she smacked my chest. "Not like that."

I gave her a dramatic frown and she snorted.

Half an hour later, Kathy and Karl showed up with Kyle. Angie sat on the patio couch with her Aunt. She gave Kyle a hard time, about the other night. He teased her about being *friends* with Ben now. She just rolled her eyes at him, even though she was trying not to laugh.

A little later, we heard more noise coming through the house. Kent showed up with his wife and two people I hadn't met yet.

"Hey, Ang?" Angie turned to Kent and looked at him. "Look who I found roaming the streets." He stepped onto the porch and another man followed behind, grinning ear to ear. He had dark brown hair and tanned skin.

"Hey, Angie."

Angie jumped up and squealed as she ran around and pounced on him. "Rob!"

Rob laughed and caught her, spinning in circles. I turned to Marcus.

"Another cousin?"

Marcus scratched his jaw, torn between laughing and being wary. "Nope. That would be Missy's older brother. He was a year ahead of Kyle and Angela in school. But the three were practically inseparable. He and Ang dated for most of it but parted as friends. Pretty sure he took my daughter's innocence too." He grumbled out the last part.

"We both had to suck that one up years ago, Marcus." A woman said with a laugh. She had black hair, the roots turning gray on her.

"Lauren. Always nice to see you." Marcus leaned over and gave her a hug. "This is an old friend of mine, Jace."

"Nice to meet you." I shook her hand, keeping one eye on Angie as she took Rob's hand and pulled him back to where she had been sitting.

I turned and flipped the burger patties, trying to look casual. "You guys live around here?"

"I do. For the last few years Rob has lived in Daytona. His company had a position open down here, so he put in the transfer."

"So, you finally have both your babies home again." Marcus leaned against the patio railing with his arms crossed in front of him.

Lauren grinned like she was the happiest woman in the world. "Yes. I'm excited to have them both close by." Her eyes moved to where Angie and the others were sitting. "Maybe I'm not the only one too."

Rob had an arm draped over the back of the couch where Angie was sitting. His eyes left no one doubting what he wanted.

"I don't know about that, Lauren. A lot of time has passed." Marcus didn't seem as happy as her about it.

"We'll see." She winked at him then turned back to me. "So, Jace. What is it that you do?"

I made small talk with her and Marcus for a few minutes. They shared stories of the times the boys got in trouble. Usually by Angie. She really did have a rep for tattling on everybody when she was younger. She earned it too.

When lunch was ready, Karl helped us carry everything to the tables I helped Marcus set up this morning. Everyone slowly made their way over. Angie sat by me, and Rob sat on her other side.

"We need to hang out soon, catch up." Rob told her. He was trying too hard to sound nonchalant about it. To my ears anyway.

"We so do. How long are you in town for?"

"Permanently. I just transferred back last week."

Angie gave a low squeal and hugged his arm. "I'm so glad. We should do something next weekend, maybe Kyle too. Just like the old days."

"Maybe, he and I haven't been able to talk much these days, conflicting schedules, and all. Kent only knew I was back because of Missy."

"Yeah, that makes sense. Kyle's been in the doghouse and hiding from everyone anyway."

Rob chuckled and wiped his face with a napkin, casting a quick look to Kyle down the way. "What did he do now?"

"Set me up with Ben under false pretenses, it was a lot of drama."

Rob grimaced. "Ben? Really?"

Angie giggled and pushed his shoulder. "He's not as bad as he used to be, still needs to work on the creep factor, but he is getting better." Rob gave her a look and she smacked him. "Only friends. He's lucky I'll accept that much."

Rob shook his head. "Still picky, huh?"

"Yep." She avoided looking at him as she dropped her hand down to the side. I reached down and she curled a finger with mine. It was small but something at least.

"Tell you what. I have to work all week, but I do need to go apartment hunting soon, preferably before mom has me picking out new paint for my old room. You wanna come with me?"

Angie took her hand back to lift up her fat burger - she wasn't picky when it came to her food that was for sure - to take a bite. She acted like she was thinking it over while chewing, then took a drink of Sprite.

"I can go Saturday, are you off?"

Rob smirked. "I'm the store manager, I don't work weekends unless I want to."

Angie giggled. "I still can't believe you went to four years of college, just to go back to your old store and manage it."

He looked a little uncomfortable as he pushed chips around his plate. "Eh. I like it there."

"You like the discount there."

"That too."

Lauren, who was sitting across from me, next to Missy and Kent, pulled my attention back. I tried to focus on her and not what Angie and her old boyfriend were talking about. Or the way he was trying to flirt with her without it looking obvious. To her at least. Lauren kept watching them with a big grin. Marcus kept watching them with a scowl.

It was a very long day by the time everyone left. Rob gave Angie a tight hug and they exchanged numbers. I went into the kitchen to clean up, not able to stomach any more of it. She joined me a few minutes later.

"Hey."

"Hey." I tipped my chin up but didn't stop cleaning.

She walked up behind me, wrapped her arms around my waist, and pressed her face against my chest.

"You alright?"

"I'm okay." She sounded tired.

I put the spoon I was washing down and turned around. She barely moved enough to let me turn.

I stroked the side of her head, running my hand down one of the braids. "You should go home and rest. I don't want you getting sick."

She turned her head and set her chin on my collarbone. "I'm fine, Jason. It's been a long day."

I cleared my throat. "Yeah, I noticed. Old boyfriend back in town."

Her arms dropped and she stepped back. "He's also a friend."

"He looked like he wanted to be more than that."

Angie scoffed and shook her head. The kind where you want to deny it. "We've been friends for a long time. We've always been close."

"Yeah." My voice sounded clipped, even to me. "I could tell. I heard all about it today too. Lauren seems to think you two are going to get back together now that he is back in town."

She rubbed her forehead with both hands and let out a low growl. "This is ridiculous. Fine. Believe what you want. I'm going home." She marched over to the patio door, said goodbye to her dad, then walked to the front door.

I cursed at myself for being a jealous idiot and jogged after her. I grabbed her hand, but she pulled away from me.

"I'm sorry, okay? I'm just lost here, Angie. Half the time I think I've lost you, then we get nights like last night, and then today… well. I don't know what to make of it."

I saw the tears brimming and reached for her again, but she took a step back. "We've talked about this."

"Your words say one thing, but then your actions say another."

She looked past me to where the backyard was. I turned around to see if Marcus was coming, but he wasn't.

"Why do you think I stay away so much? When you're close… I can't…"

This time I didn't give her a choice. I pulled on her arm and held her, kissing her head. "I know. I know."

Angie gave herself a minute, then sniffled and pushed back. What a fitting description of our relationship, push and pull. Push and pull.

"I need to go. I can't do this right now." And then she was gone.

CHAPTER 15

Angie

No more nights at dad's house. Not until Jason moved out. The fact that he hadn't yet made me wonder if he was even planning on staying. One more reason we shouldn't be together. He didn't even know what he was going to do with his life. He could up and move back to Las Vegas whenever he wanted. I knew his Uncle would be thrilled to have him home. Jason had his whole family there, waiting for him to get his head on straight.

Today was such a fun day. I forgot how easy and fun things were with Rob. Even still, I had a smidge of guilt growing inside me every time he brushed my hair back or put his arm around me. It was the way we had always been. Every time he came to town. But it wasn't him I wanted doing that anymore.

But I let him do it anyway, with Jason right there.

I barely made it through work the next few days. I couldn't tell if I was getting sick or not. There were times some food just wasn't sitting right.

It had to be all the stress. And most of that stress came from Jason. Not him per se, but more… our situation.

Whit kept telling me that dad would be fine with Jason and me being together. She was still on the what if it worked out train. Nat was in a bad place and liked to play devil's advocate. She kept telling me I needed to move on. Try someone else on for size, clean my palette.

Tempting idea, actually. Sort of. I didn't know.

I jumped when someone knocked on my door Friday night. I smiled, thinking Jason came to surprise me. The smile dropped a tiny bit when I opened the door.

"I can't believe you managed to stay in the same place for almost a decade."

I laughed. Rob had always made me laugh. "Yeah, not hard to do when I have a job that doesn't move me around all the time. What are you doing here?"

He brought a hidden arm around from his back, lifting up a to-go bag from Olive Garden. "I was in the mood for pasta and company." He scrunched up his nose in an adorable way. "It's okay, right? You don't have any other plans?"

I laughed and moved out of the way. "Get in here, you idiot."

"Ah. Someone is hungry. Guess I have good timing."

I closed the door and followed him to the dining room. He hadn't been there in years, but he still remembered the way.

"Shut up and feed me."

He pulled a foil container out with a flourish, then handed me a fork. While he unloaded the rest of the bag, I dug into my meatball marinara pasta. With the first bite I closed my eyes and hummed happily. When I opened them again, Rob was staring at me.

"What?"

He shook his head, like he was clearing his thoughts. "Nothing. I take it, I chose well?"

I nodded, shoving in another bite. "This is exactly what I needed tonight, thank you."

Rob turned in his chair, so we were facing each other, but still on the same side of the table.

"How was work? Are you adjusting to the new store?"

"Yeah. It's fine. The usual awkwardness around the new boss, but that's about it. Feels kind of weird being back where I started though."

"Lots of memories in that place." I grinned, reaching over to grab a breadstick.

He chuckled. "I still can't pass the fitting rooms without blushing."

I paused with the breadstick halfway to my mouth. "I can imagine." I was the one blushing now. I set the breadstick down, one end in my pasta and covered my face. "That is so embarrassing. I can't believe we did that."

Rob just laughed. "Shoot, I can. I don't regret it for a minute."

I screamed into my hands, making him laugh harder. "Of course, you don't. You're a guy."

Rob reached up and peeled my fingers down. "We didn't do anything wrong."

I dropped my hands, my eyes on them as he folded our fingers together. "We could have gotten in so much trouble though."

"Yeah." His voice was getting a bit croaky, he cleared it and pulled his hand back. "It's a good thing Kyle never knew."

"Oh my gosh, right? He would have been the first person to tell, just so he could pay me back. I must say, getting him in trouble was one of my favorite pastimes."

"I noticed. I think the best part was the time he was in the store with us. He had no clue." Rob leaned over and bopped my nose. "And you liked playing with fire."

I straightened my back and put on an air of indifference. "I did not. It was just fun to get away with things he couldn't."

"Only because you didn't let him."

I shrugged. "Someone had too."

"You also used it as a way to cover up for us. Like the time he found us in the closet together during a movie night with him and Kent. He got so excited, thinking he was finally going to get one on you."

I laughed and covered my mouth to keep my food where it belonged. "He just forgot he had one of Uncle Karl's beers in his hands. The second they walked in the door, he opened his mouth, but I was faster." I bent over laughing, trying to swallow and not choke. "His mom and dad wouldn't let him say anything in rebuttal."

Rob was laughing nearly as hard as I was. "I thought for sure your dad was going to come after me with a shotgun that night."

I nodded, laughing so hard that tears started coming out of my eyes. We ate in silence for a few minutes, finishing our dinner, and getting our breathing evened out.

"We had a lot of fun together. What happened?" Rob turned, leaning down onto his knees. "What happened to us, Ang?"

I combed his hair with my fingers. "You know what happened. And then you left for college. Then I left. You never came back, but I did."

"There was a time when I thought you and I would always be it." I nodded. I had thought the same. Hell, we talked about it. "I never planned on being gone for so long, I swear."

"I know. That's just how life goes. You had a life in Daytona, one you liked. I have a life here. One I love. I never faulted you for living the life you wanted."

"And now?" He brought his head up, desperation bleeding through his eyes.

I tilted my head. "And now, what?" Where was he going with this?

"My life is here now. I asked Kyle, he said you weren't seeing anyone. I miss you, Ang. I miss us."

Oh. Well. Shiitake mushrooms (Laura made us all cut back on our cursing), Jason was right.

"I... I don't know, Rob." I did know, but he made some good points. We had been good together. Why did he have to come back now? Why couldn't he have come back months ago? Before I took that trip to Vegas.

He reached forward and grabbed my hands, our heads nearly touching now. "It's okay, just give me a chance. Please?"

"I... uh."

"Please, Ang. I need you." Dang it. I was a sucker for that sad pitiful look, and he knew it.

"Maybe?"

He grinned. "I can work with a maybe." He leaned back into his chair, releasing my hands. "Ready for dessert?"

"Depends. What'd you bring me?"

He chuckled and opened another box. My eyes widened.

"Chocolate Brownie Lasagna." He picked up a fork and slid the side of it down, scooping a forkful, then holding it up. "Come on, you know you want some."

That sounded wrong and he knew it. Still, I couldn't resist the chocolatey goodness. I leaned forward, opening my mouth. I hummed greedily as soon as I tasted it.

"See, some things never change. I still know your sweet spots."

I blushed and leaned back, the food turning into a brick as it went down my throat. For some reason he took it as an invitation. He fell to his knees in front of me and pulled my neck closer. I let him. His lips barely had to touch mine for me to know. This wasn't what I wanted. *He* wasn't what I wanted. No matter what kind of past we had. It was just that, the past.

"I will get you to trust me again, Ang." He kissed my forehead and stood up. "I'll see you in the morning."

I let him leave without a word. Then I changed into sweats, grabbed a blanket, and the rest of my dessert. I cuddled with a pillow on my couch, stuffed my face, and watched Hallmark. And yeah, balled my freaking eyes out.

Once the food was gone, I sat there, holding my phone, Jason's contact information covering my screen. I had long ago put the picture of us at the airport, collecting his winnings, as his contact picture.

To call him or not to call him. That was the question.

I caved… and went to bed. Then I woke up in the middle of the night to puke, brush my teeth, and go back to sleep. This was really getting ridiculous. One thing was for sure, I wasn't eating chocolate again for a while. I ended up brushing my teeth again first thing in the morning and gargling with mouthwash. Twice.

I felt slightly human again by the time Rob showed up. Carrying donuts. I covered my mouth as soon as the scent hit my nose.

"Hey, you all right?"

"Yeah, I probably just ate too much last night. My stomach has been sensitive this morning. Thank you, though. This was sweet of you." I stepped into another room, as though to get my purse, but really needing a clean breath of air.

Rob put the food on the counter and followed me. I picked up my bag and grabbed my keys off my dresser.

"Are you sure you're alright? You look a little pale."

I pasted on my fake smile. Something I was getting a lot of practice with lately. "I'm fine. It's already passing. You ready to go?"

"Sure." He didn't sound like it, but we left anyway.

We spent the next few hours hitting up different apartment complexes. Rob found a few he liked and took applications for, but he didn't make a decision. By lunch time, I was tired and hungry.

"And you call me picky?" I asked, somewhat teasing, somewhat not. I shuffled through a few brochures that were on our table at lunch.

"I'd hate to get stuck somewhere for a year or so that I don't like." He reached over and started playing with my fingers. "Then again, that would give me a reason to hang out at your place more."

"Smooth." I smirked.

He grinned, folding our fingers completely together.

"It wouldn't be as good as sneaking into fitting rooms, or coat closets, or… the shower stalls in the locker room after practice."

I cringed. "We weren't exactly picky with where we made out, were we?"

Rob lifted my fingers to kiss them. "Not just make out." Cue the blush here. "It's not like we had much time alone when we were at each other's houses."

"No, we did not. It was like my dad had a sixth sense for when you were over, and in my room." Huh, he seemed to have lost that sense. Otherwise, Jason would be dead by now.

"Imagine it, freedom to do what we want. When we want. As *loud* as we want." His voice dropped deeper, but he kept it smooth.

It wasn't hard to imagine. I just had to think of all the times that Jason was over, and we did just that. Speaking of which, I could really use a good massage again.

"I'm starting to think this whole apartment hunting thing was a ruse. You are not moving in with me, Rob." I smiled, trying to make it sound like I was teasing. In reality, I was mildly panicking.

He let go of my hand, sitting back with a laugh. "You seem like you are feeling better now."

"A little, but I may still keep it light for lunch."

It didn't work. By the time we made it back to my little bungalow, I was running for the bathroom. Rob, being the gentleman that he was, held my hair. And even handed me a washcloth to clean up.

I moaned out a whimper and laid down on the cool tile floor.

"You know what this reminds me of?"

I glared at him, not in the mood for any more reminiscing. He carried on anyway because he was obviously a man with an agenda.

"This reminds me of the time we got into Karl's liquor cabinet. The first time, not the time you ratted on Kyle. Actually, I think you threw him under the table for that one too."

Dang, that one was a good memory.

"You only had a few bottles, but you spent the night puking then too. You were such a lightweight back then." Okay, that wasn't the good part of it. We had a lot of fun before that part of the night.

"Still am, that's why I rarely drink."

He chuckled, shaking his head, and leaned down to help me up. "Come on, let's get you to bed."

"Seriously?"

He laughed, supporting most of my weight. "That was not what I meant, and you know it. While I *will* get you back in bed, I'd rather wait until you aren't sick."

"I'm too tired to argue with that claim." I mumbled, letting him lead the way.

He kissed my cheek as we came to a stop by my bed. "If I promise to behave, could I help you change? Technically, I have seen it all before. I mean, you have definitely gotten better with age, but you are still the same."

I just closed my eyes and pretended he was Jason, as he slid my jeans down. I stopped him before the shirt came off too.

"The bra?"

"I can handle that much, thank you." I opened one eye to glare at him at least a little bit.

"Are you sure? I don't mind, really." I kept the glare steady. His straight face wasn't as steady. "Can I at least unsnap it for you?"

With a huff, I turned and put my back to him. He lifted my shirt greedily and released the stupid thing. Then kissed my back softly, as he slid his hands up and began to push the straps down. I stepped away and finished the job by myself. Then climbed in bed. I passed out soon after.

I woke up sometime later, to the sounds of the television. I pulled my robe on and walked out. Rob saw me and paused the movie before walking over to me.

"Hey. Feeling any better?"

"Yeah, I think so. You're still here?"

He looked confused. "Did you not want me to be? I told you, I'm in this babe. I want to take care of you."

Dang it. Now I felt like crying. He was being too sweet. Rob obviously had no idea what to do, so he just settled for helping me to the couch.

"Do you want water? Toast? Soup?"

I patted the seat next to me on the couch and he sat down. I laid down and put my head on his lap. Without a pause, he started brushing my hair back with his fingers. This was something we had done a thousand times in the past. Something natural and comforting.

I slept on and off the rest of the day. At some point, he moved me back to the bed, and laid down with me, just holding me. They weren't the arms I wanted, but they were at least familiar.

The next morning, I started the process all over again. Rob insisted on staying, and he even called my dad to explain I couldn't make it to dinner. I was really hoping to kick this sucker in the butt before Monday. We were only a month into the new school year, it was too soon to start using sick days.

CHAPTER 16

Jason

"Hey, Kyle." I greeted the younger man as I climbed out of my truck after lunch on Friday.

We were on a new site this week. One of Marcus' regular clients had hired us to build a guest house in their backyard. More than a few times I would close my eyes and would feel like I was back in that desert. It felt good to find some similarities between my two lives. It made every day feel just a little bit easier.

"Hey, Jace. Have a good lunch?"

"It was fine. Just hid in a corner in a Wendy's and enjoyed the air conditioning." While most of the world was starting to cool down, we weren't. Especially those of us working in the sun all day. "How was yours?"

"Pretty good. Met up with Rob." Kyle grinned. "It's cool having him back again. Just like the good old days."

I chuckled. "I get that. Felt the same way when I first got to your Uncle's place." Kyle nodded, like this made all the sense in the world. "How's he like being back?"

"He loves it, he doesn't know why he didn't come back sooner. I think part of him was afraid too."

"Why? He has family and friends here. Everyone seemed happy to see him." Especially Angie.

Oh. That was probably why.

As though he heard me, he nodded. "Yeah, Ang. They were really tight back in the day, and I think he kind of freaked, which is why he left. Then he was too afraid to come back and man up."

I swallowed and set my tool box down on the workbench we were using. I never left my set lying around. It had been through hell and back with me. Literally.

"Is that why he is back then? Angie?"

Kyle shrugged and picked up his tool belt. "Maybe. He asked lots of questions at lunch. He's planning to surprise her with dinner tonight, and one of her favorite desserts." Kyle laughed to himself. "He's gonna try his luck. See if he can get her to remember all the good times first, then try to convince her they'd be good together again."

I set the ladder up, trying to make it look like I wasn't as interested as I was. "And would they be?"

I climbed up as he picked up a handful of shingles to start handing them up to me.

"I don't know, to be honest. They haven't been together since high school. That was like fifteen years ago. People change. But, seeing as neither of them have been in a serious relationship since, maybe. They were practically glued to each other's hips back then. Or lips.

Whichever. He came back to visit a few times, even helped us move her into her house. I think he stayed the night, but I'm not sure. Anyway, he seems to have come home with a mission. To get his girl back. Problem is. I'm not sure she's his anymore."

I froze in the middle of setting the handful he'd just handed me down. "Whose is she then?"

Kyle climbed up the ladder until he was closer to me. I finally set my load down and looked at him.

"You probably know that better than I do."

"I'm not sure I know what you are talking about, Kyle."

"Last month, on the first day we checked out her roof. I came back to see if you needed help with anything. Saw more than I was meant to in that little kitchen of hers. At least I was early enough that I didn't have to pour Clorox over my eyes."

I pinched my eyes closed and dropped my head.

"I don't know what's going on between you and my cousin. Frankly, I don't want to know, either. But I do know her. And I have only ever seen her look at one other person the way she looks at you. He left her. She said she was fine with it. But it doesn't change the fact that he left her high and dry. It did something to her. Rob was the person who put her back together after her mom died. They had met a few times before that when Uncle Marcus brought them home to visit. But the moment she moved back, permanently, it was his arms that held her together. And then he left. That does something to someone's psyche. It makes them cling to what they have. It makes them afraid to take important people away from those they care about. She just needs a little encouragement."

He stepped down two rungs then looked back up. "Just don't take too long. If she doesn't think she has you, she will settle for him. He knows the buttons to push, he knows her. Probably better than anyone. Except you. He only knows the past Angie, not the current one. Not who she is now."

That was a lot to unpack, but what I took from it was that I better move my butt before I lost her to the past. Kyle's insight made her comments the other night make more sense as well.

Angie had only ever known the military lifestyle. Then her mom died suddenly, in front of her. Her dad got his discharge, and moved them across the country, to Florida. To live near people she had only seen on occasion. So, she fell for the one kid that could make her happy. Then life happened and he left her too.

Was she afraid of me leaving her? Or me leaving Marcus? Or her dad pushing her away?

Only one thing truly stayed with me. Angie was protecting herself as much as anyone else in this. She was afraid of change. And us being together would cause a major shift in dynamics. But in a good way, right?

Kyle let me work in silence, probably knowing my mind was elsewhere. Part of me wanted to beat Rob to her house tonight. To stake my claim, officially. But she wasn't ready for that. Or was she?

Would my pushing her, push her away? Did he stand a chance? If he did, did that mean she never really got over him?

What if she really had been waiting for him to come all this time? She was pretty happy to see him the other day.

I decided to give him this one weekend. I could see what her thoughts were about it all on Sunday. By then, she would know what he was after. She would know if she wanted a second chance with him. If she didn't, *then* I would start pushing her.

I ended up running that night, not being able to sit still long enough to watch a movie or play cards with Marcus. He didn't even question it. Which was good. I wouldn't know how to answer him anyway.

Was Rob over there now? Was he filling her head with those memories?

I was sure he was the one she referred to, when she told me about the fitting rooms. Would those memories make her remember how she used to feel about him?

I tossed and turned most of that night. I stared at my phone, going back and forth on whether I should contact her. Was she still feeling under the weather? She didn't look so great the other night. Not that I helped much with that.

Maybe I should check on her.

Saturday was a long day. I was up and running before dawn.

Were they apartment hunting? Were they breaking in his new place? Did he stay the night?

Marcus' grill ended up getting a good scrub. And I mowed his lawn. He just sat back on his couch, feet propped up, flipping through channels on the tv.

I ran again before bed. Showered. Then just laid there.

Sunday morning, I waited on pins and needles. Would she come early again?

Around four, Marcus finally broke his silence by answering the phone.

"Hey, buttercup… Oh, sorry, Rob. Why are you using Angela's phone?"

Good question.

"Oh. Oh, yeah, that'll do it… Alright. Tell her I love her, and I'll call her tomorrow to check on her." He hung up the phone and went back to channel surfing.

If I didn't know any better, I'd say he was torturing me on purpose. Payback for all the very naughty things I'd done to his daughter, under his own roof even.

"Angie not coming tonight?" It was a lot of work to keep my voice emotionless.

"Nope. Looks like she was getting sick after all. Rob said it started Friday night, but really hit home yesterday afternoon. He said not to worry, he's taking care of her. He was always good at taking care of her. Until he wasn't." Marcus seemed as thrilled as I did by this turn of events.

"You don't sound very happy about this. At least she isn't alone."

He huffed. "No. And that's the only reason I'm not going to get mad at him. He cares for her, I know that. But I *don't* think he is what's best for her. Not for my girl."

I turned my head to look at him. "Why? What is best for her?"

He looked back at me and gave me that look. The one that called me an idiot and said he wanted to smack me. Then he turned back to the tv, flipping through another stupid channel.

So, she let Rob stay with her. Had he been there since Friday? Had he been holding her? Taking care of her? Doing *my* job?

I pushed off the couch. "I'm going for a run."

"Yep." That was all I got out of him.

I caved that night and messaged her.

Me: Are you okay?

It took a few minutes, but her response did eventually come.

Angie: Yeah. Just a stomach flu. Already passing.
Me: Did he stay the whole time?
Angie: He just left. He only stayed last night.
Angie: Nothing happened besides me sleeping and puking.

I released the breath I'd been holding since my talk with Kyle.

Me: Can I come see you?
Angie: I'm not exactly up for company.

And yet Rob spent the weekend with her.

Me: Got it. Feel better.
Angie: Jason…
Me: No, I get it. Get some sleep.

I silenced my phone and plugged it in. I left it on the carpeted floor, where I wouldn't hear the vibrations if she responded.

I saw a half a dozen missed messages from her the next morning. All of which I deleted without reading them. She made her choice. I didn't need to hear her excuses. Not again.

Kyle and I hardly spoke throughout the next week. I hardly spoke to anybody. As much as I liked it here, it was becoming obvious that I was going to need to move on soon. I couldn't stay here and watch her be happy with him. I wished Angie all the happiness in the world, she deserved it. I just couldn't watch it.

Friday night, I finally approached Marcus.

He was sitting at the kitchen table, reading the newspaper. He was weird like that, he preferred to read it after the day was over. I stood behind one of the chairs, gripping the back of it.

"Hey, can we talk for a minute?"

He lowered the paper with a sad sigh. "How long until you bail?"

That brought me up short. "How'd you know that was what I was going to say?"

He shrugged. "In the infantry you are taught to watch and observe. We think before we act. You've been getting more and more restless lately. I did too. I went through a phase I wasn't sure how to get out of."

I pulled the chair out and sat down. "How did you?"

"Simple, I realized I had to make a choice. The right one will help you find a balance. The wrong one will send you into a tailspin. I chose wrong at first. I hid it from Ang, but I went out a lot in the beginning. I thought maybe I just needed to replace Marta, that I needed to move on. I had more one-night stands than I care to admit. I got worse. And worse. Then, one morning, I woke up in someone else's bed. No memory of who they were or what we did. The only thing I did know was that I had left my baby girl alone with no warning. And no way to contact me. My phone had died sometime in the night too. I practically ran home, and found her sleeping in my bed, holding a bear I gave her mother when we were dating. Right then and there, I realized I chose the wrong path. I curled in that bed with my girl, and I held her tight. I haven't let go since. Nor have I been unbalanced since."

"Is that why you don't like to go out anymore?"

"Partly. Mostly it was because I felt like I was betraying Marta. She's been gone for almost twenty years, and I still feel guilty for even looking at another woman. The only way I slept with anyone during that time was when I was as drunk as a Navy man on shore leave."

I snorted, then frowned. "How do I know which is the right course for me?"

"Simple, find what makes you happy. What brings you peace. That's all you have to do. And when you find it, you hold to it with every ounce of strength in your body."

That was my problem though. What brought me peace was the same thing that brought him peace. Just in a different way. And that course was no longer open to me.

"When you're ready to talk to me about what is sending you through this tailspin, let me know. I will *always* be here to talk to you. If you feel like leaving is what you need to do, I understand. The room will be here when you come to your senses."

I smirked at the Know It All and pushed back from the table, I paused at the doorway that led from the kitchen and dining area to the rest of the house.

"Oh, I've been meaning to ask. Have you heard from Angie? Is she feeling better?"

I could see a smile wanting to come out. "Yes. She says she is fine. Her stomach has still been on the sensitive side, making her not want to eat. But Rob has been coming over every night, practically force feeding her."

"Well, I'm glad she has him then."

Marcus snorted in sarcastic amusement and turned back to his paper.

I walked back up the stairs to call my uncle. We had another barbeque planned for Marcus' birthday next week. As his birthday fell on a Thursday this year, we were planning it for Saturday. I would stay at least that long.

After talking to my Uncle, I made plane reservations for the day after. I used Marcus' printer and printed up the receipt/ticket. I hated trying to find the digital copy when I got to the airport to check in. This was easier. I stuck it in the corner of the mirror that sat on top of the dresser, that way I wouldn't lose it.

Sunday morning, I packed my backpack and told Marcus I was going hiking. There was no way I was going to be able to be around Angie. And if Rob had been with her every day, odds were that he would be coming too.

I knew I needed to tell her that I was leaving, but I could wait until the party. With lots of people around.

CHAPTER 17

Angie

Monday morning, I was feeling almost normal again. Just to be safe, I only ate toast for breakfast. Rob insisted I drink a glass of apple juice with it. He stayed with me all weekend, making sure I was taken care of.

I lied to Jason, and that thought killed me. But I knew he already knew Rob was here before that. I was sure that my dad told him that Rob was taking care of me. Jason didn't need to know that he was still here.

I couldn't very well kick Rob out just so he could come either. Not after everything Rob had done for me the last few days. I tried to explain that to Jason, I even admitted he was still there. But he never responded. I felt the fissure spread from one side of my heart to the next. He was giving up on me.

Just like I told him to. How many times did I tell him we couldn't be together? And now was when he chose to finally back off?

"Are you sure you should be going to work today?" Rob asked for the fiftieth time.

"Yes. I feel fine. The toast seems to be settling fine." I snapped, then softened my tone when I saw his worried look. I walked over and gave him a hug. "Thank you, but I promise, I feel better."

He hugged me back with a defeated sigh. "I will keep my phone on me all day. Call me if you need me. And I will pick up some soup from that Cuban place down the street after work."

"Rob, you don't have to do that." I released him, but he didn't release me.

"I know. I want to. I want to take care of you. I can't tell you how long I have felt guilty for leaving you like I did. We could have been married by now. Maybe even had a couple kids." He slid his hand forward and rubbed my belly softly.

We both froze at the same time.

"Angie, is it possible?"

My breathing started picking up. "No, I mean, yes, I guess it's always possible. I'm on the pill, but that's not exactly fool proof, is it?"

I expected him to recoil away from me, not hold me tighter and kiss my head.

"When was your last period?"

My laugh probably sounded a little crazy. "I don't know. You know I have never been regular like that. They come and go as they please."

"Okay, but do you remember how long ago the last one was?"

I laid my head on his shoulder, letting him comfort me.

"Um, before Vegas, maybe?"

"Okay, and that was how long ago?"

"End of July, beginning of Aug."

"So, you may not have had a period in at least two months?"

"Yes. But I've been known to skip a month here and there." I pushed away from him, straightening my clothes, and forced myself to focus. "No. I doubt I am pregnant. I've been stressed lately, I got sick. That's it. Now, I need to go."

"Ang…"

"No, Rob. I'm not pregnant. I'm not." My voice cracked. "I have to leave or I'm going to be late. Thank you for your help." Without thinking, I leaned in and kissed him. "Ugh, sorry. Don't know where that came from."

He chuckled shyly. "I do. You're falling into us again, just like me."

I shook my head and picked up my computer bag and purse. "Nope. Cannot deal with this right now."

He followed me out of the house, that big stupid grin still on his face. He walked me all the way to my car, kissing me again before I could get in.

"Have a good day at work, sweetheart."

I glared at him and got in.

It was a very long day at work.

Rob had packed me a small sandwich for lunch, in case I felt like eating anything. One smell of it told me that was not going to happen. And that something else may have.

This could not be happening! Why?

My brain just couldn't process any of this. It had been too much already. So much so that I started bawling in my classroom. I barely held myself together once the kiddos came back. But I did.

I robotically put my things away when I got home, changed into a pair of pajama shorts and a tank top, without the bra. Were they actually sore, or was that just my imagination running wild? Either way, the bra had bugged me all day.

I hadn't locked the door, so Rob just walked inside after knocking. He set his own computer bag on my small loveseat, and then sat on the coffee table in front of me. I just blinked at him. He leaned in and kissed me softly. I didn't move or respond.

"I take it we have passed the land of impossibility and denial?"

I blinked again, this time soaking my eyelashes.

"Oh, sweetheart. You're not alone in this. I promise. I will be right here, by your side the whole time."

"If I am pregnant, then this is obviously not your kid. We haven't slept together in seven years, Rob."

"I know that. But it should have been mine. It would have been had I not chickened out the last time you had this scare." He cupped my head, hair and all, kissing my forehead. "I will never forgive myself for that."

"I wasn't pregnant, Rob. You were 18, I was 17. We didn't know then that I was irregular. Mix that with a real stomach flu, and we both flipped."

"Yes, but I am the one that ran away from you. I loved you, with all my heart. I planned to spend the rest of my life with you, but that pregnancy scare made the reality of it all sink in so much faster, so much deeper. I've grown a lot since then, Ang. I'm not leaving you again."

"And what about the father? The actual, biological father?"

He grimaced, obviously not wanting to think about the fact that I was sleeping with someone else just weeks ago.

"You aren't with him anymore. If he wants to be a part of our baby's life, then so be it. If not, I will sign the birth certificate."

"How can you say all this when we've hardly spoken in years? Even after the last time you visited, you stopped calling altogether. How can this be so much different?"

"Because I don't want to be without you anymore. I've never stopped loving you, Ang. And it has never stopped terrifying me. A few months ago, I was dating someone, and she pointed out that I was never actually with her. It's always been you. I came home because I want my girl back."

"And what if I want someone else?"

He let go of me and slid back, his eyes wide. He almost looked like I kicked him in the nuts. I would know, because I have, and he gave me that same look. A mix of pain and betrayal.

"Do you?" He finally gasped out. "Am I too late?"

I shrugged, suddenly feeling very shy and uncomfortable talking about this. "I don't know. Things got more complicated than either of us were expecting. I'm pretty sure I love him, but I don't see how it would work out. Not without destroying a lot of people's lives."

"I don't understand. How could it destroy lives? He's not married is he?"

That time I did kick him. Unfortunately, he knew me well enough that he was able to intercept my foot.

"I'm not suggesting you would do such a thing. I'm just trying to make sense of it all."

I sighed and stood up. "I know. I have been doing the same all day. I really should have picked up a test before I came home. None of this matters if I'm not pregnant."

Rob stood up, wiping his hands on his black suit pants, and cleared his throat. "I, uh, picked one up during my lunch today."

I spun back around; not sure I heard him right. "You, what?"

He scratched his head, reminding me of the adorably shy little boy I met so long ago. He opened his mouth, then closed it and bent down to his bag. He pulled out a small pink box and handed it to me.

"I figured you would come around eventually and would want one. I thought I would play it safe and get it for you."

I reached tentatively for it; afraid it would bite me. I held it in much the same manner too. Slowly, I walked the plank to my bathroom, taking deep breaths before I took the plunge. Never in my life did I expect to be doing this twice. Oddly, the first time I was excited. Terrified out of my wits, but excited. I had Rob back then. I had no doubts that he would be with me.

Now, I was terrified again. And Rob was right outside the bathroom, probably pacing again too. This time though, it wasn't him that put me there. And it wasn't him I wanted by my side. But, just like last time, I knew he would be.

I washed my hands slowly, drawing out the time. Once they were thoroughly germ free, and dry, I went back to the test. I didn't pick it up. I just left it sitting there on the counter. I took two steps out the door and crumbled.

Rob ran over and sat with me in my hallway, letting me cry it all out. In time, I let him help me to the bed, I laid there, and let him hold me. At least I wasn't alone.

When the sobs finally seemed to be at bay, he started talking again.

"I will be here, Ang. In whatever capacity you will take me in."

"Even if I love someone else?"

He chuckled softly. "Sweetheart, I already got you to fall in love with me once before. Even after I left you, it never took much to get you on your back." I punched him in the side, and he laughed. "If you give me the chance, I will prove myself worthy of your love again."

"I do, a little bit. I always have. But it still wouldn't be fair to you."

He shrugged. "I'm not worried about it. But first, I need to know who the father is. He needs a choice in all this too."

I rolled to my back, needing a little space.

"Ang, sweetheart. I can't help you through this if I don't know what happened. Trust me. I would rather tell everyone this is my baby and pretend he never happened. But it did. Please just trust me."

I sat up and turned to face him, crossing my legs under me. "You might see me differently for it."

He moved to box me in his legs again, putting his hands on mine. "We took each other's virginity in a dressing room. Do your worst."

"When I was flying back from Vegas, Hurricane Edith was passing through. My flight got delayed." I went through and told him the story of how I met Jason. Not every detail, mind you.

"So, you what, decided to pass the time in the bathroom?"

I shook my head, laughing softly, and a bit sarcastically. "No. Nothing really happened. But I did see him again that night." I looked right into his eyes for this part. "At my dad's house."

He crossed his eyes and tilted his head. "Why would he be there?"

I licked my lips and rubbed them together. "Because he had just left the Marines and my dad had invited him to come work with him. To help him transition to civilian life."

Rob got quiet, eerily quiet. I started to move away, but he gripped my hands tighter. So, I stayed. I waited.

"Jace?"

"Yeah. That would be him."

"This makes so much sense, now." His voice took on that light bulb moment quality.

"What does?"

"Labor day, the barbecue. He was always nearby, always looking like he was ready to stab me with something. I didn't get it. I just figured he was a cranky guy. Your dad had been pretty scary when he first came home too."

I smiled. "Yeah, uh. We've both been thrown into blind dates a few times. Neither of us liked it much seeing the other with someone else."

"Then why aren't you together? He isn't as old as your dad, is he?" Rob leaned back. To an outsider he probably looked grossed out. But I knew he was just trying to get a better read on me.

"No. He is eight years younger than my dad. Fourteen years older than me."

"Okay, so age wasn't the problem."

I giggled. "You remember his rule?"

He huffed. "Are you kidding? How can I forget? I finally worked up the nerve to ask you out, and your response was to ask how old I was. Since I was a year older, you said yes. Then I come to pick you up, and you dad grills me down to my birth date."

I giggled. "Yeah, he's funny like that."

"Funny-scary. So, what is it then? What's stopping you?"

"Dad hasn't said anything, but I know he still misses military life. He's missed all of his buddies. He and Jason kept in touch. The minute dad found out they gave Jason an ultimatum, dad told him to come here. Dad has been so happy too. He sacrificed so much to make sure I had a stable home and at least one parent with me. I couldn't take Jason away from him."

Rob's laugh started out slow, then grew bigger until he was practically barking. I tried to push away in disgust for being laughed at, but he pulled me in for a hug.

"Oh, sweetheart. You're so cute. Trust me, your dad is not going to care. He knows Jason better than anyone else. I doubt your dad would have anything to do with someone he wouldn't approve of."

"I guess it doesn't matter anymore anyway. Jason is mad at me." I explained the text message from the night before and what I think it means.

"Yeah, but when you tell him about the baby, he will change his mind."

I scoffed and this time he let me up when I pushed him. I stepped away from the bed and folded my arms. "Right, that's just what every girl dreams of. A man to only be with her because he knocked her up."

Rob slid to the edge of the bed and grabbed my hands again. I forgot how touchy feely he was.

"Look, I doubt he has gotten over you that fast. It's been more than ten years, and you still hold my heart. Talk to him, feel him out. If he is only in it for the baby, you don't have to be. Again, I will be right here with you."

I sniffled, the tears beginning to fall again. "And if he wants nothing to do with it? This will still mess up his and my dad's relationship."

Rob stood up, tipping my chin up to look in my eyes. "No. If that happens, then we tell your dad this is *my* baby." He lifted my tank top and placed a hand on my belly again.

"You just got back a few days ago. No one will believe I am this far along already."

"So, we tell your dad I was the man you met at the airport. You said you only told him about making a new friend, right?" I nodded. "Then we tell him it was me. The complications we experienced were because I was still in Daytona. Which is why I suddenly decided to move back home. Because I finally realized I couldn't be without you."

"You'd really be willing to do all that for me?"

"Yeah, Ang. I'd do anything for you." He blinked his eyes closed then looked at the ceiling. "How do you still not see what the rest of us do?"

"Because I am nothing special. Minus the slightly serious cherry allergy."

Rob growled and held me tight. "You are special in so many ways, Angie. I used to be able to help you see that." He sighed. "I guess it's my fault that you lost sight of it. I left you."

I laid my head on his chest again, spent from the emotional roller coaster. He was content to just hold me there.

"What do you want, Ang? You've worried about everyone else. But what about you?"

"I don't know. I'm pretty sure I love him. But then you are here now. And then there is the baby. And… I don't really know anymore. I just know that I am tired. So, very tired."

"I have an idea, just go along with it."

I moved away, as far as he would let me, wary all of a sudden. "The last time you said that to me, I lost my virginity."

He barked out a laugh, then kissed me right under my ear. He kept his voice soft. "Are you saying you regretted it?"

I scoffed at the notion. "Obviously not if we repeated it a few times."

He hummed. His lips began moving along my skin in a way he knew I liked. I tensed up, and he rubbed his hand softly on my back.

"Just go with it, Angie. If you really want me to stop, you know I will."

His lips skimmed down my neck, then back up. His hand slid down to my butt, gripping me tight. He hummed with approval. His other hand slowly started making its way up my side, pushing the small shirt up.

His lips met mine the same time this thumb skimmed over the top, moving the shirt completely out of the way. I was just tender enough that it felt really good. Which then had me opening my own lips.

Rob shifted us so my back was to the bed. He leaned forward, making me fall backward. Soon, I was lying on my back, and his lips were tracing down again. About the time they reached that new tenderness, awareness came back to me.

He was Rob, not Jason. The guilt hit me like a ton of bricks. "Stop. Rob. Stop."

His lips came back to mine, his other hand pushing my shorts down. Apparently I was sensitive somewhere else too. "Are you sure that's what you want?" He asked against my lips. "Because it doesn't feel like it is."

I whimpered as my legs began to shake. "Can't."

"Can."

I whimpered again. An image of Jason doing this same thing flashed in my mind. My knee came up on its own.

Rob rolled to my side, in a ball, semi-laughing.

"Guess you know your answer." He gasped out.

I jumped up, wanting to help, but not sure how. I settled for fixing my clothes and apologizing profusely. It was a good five minutes before he could stand up straight. And I apologized again.

"Will you stop?" Even his laugh still sounded breathless. "I knew the dangers of what I was getting into. Do you know what you want, now?"

"Yeah. I mean. Obviously, I wanted to be with you. But at the same time, it felt like I was cheating on Jason."

I could tell he was disappointed by that, but not surprised. "Well, then I will just have to wait until you talk to him, then. If, for some stupid reason, he is blind and doesn't want you, with or without the baby, then I will be here. Alright?"

"How is that fair to you?"

He shrugged. "That's my problem. I left. Kyle warned me the other day that I might be too late. I thought he meant that you might have just given up on me. Now I'm wondering if he knew about the two of you."

"Maybe. He told Ben he thought something was going on between us. Ben didn't believe my lies either."

Rob started moving around a little more, purposely playing it up to make me laugh.

"Now what do I do?"

"First, you need to eat. I can walk down and pick up the soup. And then, we plan how you will tell Jace about the baby."

CHAPTER 18

Angie

All week, Rob stayed at my place. He didn't want to leave me alone. I still got sick on and off. But now that I knew what it was, I knew I wasn't going to pass it on to anyone else. Every night I tried calling Jason, every night he ignored me. Which usually meant I cried myself to sleep in Rob's arms. Not that he complained at all.

I still felt a little guilty that he was there, offering to be with me while I was crying over someone else, and planning to be with someone else, but not enough to send him away. He was the only person I had to talk to about this. I hadn't yet told my old roomies. I wasn't ready for that.

Rob and I agreed that in person would be the best way to break the news. And since Jason was refusing to communicate with me, that left one choice. Sunday dinner. Rob volunteered to come with me, so he could pull dad away and give Jason and me a few minutes alone.

By Sunday, I was a nervous wreck. Rob kept rubbing my arms and trying to say all sorts of crap to soothe me. I let him drive, as my hands were too shaky. I pulled it together enough to walk into my dad's house with a somewhat real smile.

"Hi, daddy." I walked straight to his arms. They were more comforting than Rob's.

"Hey, buttercup. How are you feeling?"

"Better."

He looked over my shoulder, a small grumble coming from him. "I see you brought Rob with you."

"Yeah, he's been staying in one of my extra rooms, so he doesn't have to stay with Lauren. He's like a lost puppy. I was afraid he would chew the furniture if I left him alone at home. You don't mind, do you?"

My dad chuckled and kissed my head. "Not at all. There was a time when it was always the two of you. If one was here, the other was sure to follow." He reached over and shook Rob's hand, welcoming him.

While he did that, I looked around the room, but didn't see any sign of Jason. "I think I left something in my room the last time I was here. I'm just going to run upstairs and see if I can find it."

Rob squeezed my hand as I passed, a silent good luck.

I jogged softly up the stairs, in a hurry to get this over with. I knocked softly, twisting the knob. Seeing as it was unlocked, I crept into Jason's room. It was dark, and again, no sign of him. Feeling defeated, I turned to leave, but a paper on his mirror caught my eye. With the dresser right next to the door, I didn't even have to reach for it. I flipped on the switch to see better, as the familiar logo at the top had me on the verge of hyperventilating.

I only needed a few words to understand. A few words for my heart to break.

He was leaving me.

I read it over again quietly, multiple times, just in case. I couldn't tear my eyes off it. I needed those repetitions for all the details to sink in.

"One week from today." I whispered. "That rat bas…"

"Angie?" Rob called, climbing to the top of the stairs, interrupting my rant before it could start. I waited for him to come to me.

"He's leaving me."

Rob stepped into the room and looked around. "How do you know?"

I pointed at the paper. "He's already made the plans. I bet he went somewhere else today. He is avoiding telling me."

"Let's go home. You're in no shape for this tonight."

I nodded mutely and let him lead me away.

"What's wrong?" My dad asked. Somewhere in my blank head, I recognized that he didn't sound all that worried or concerned. Not the way he normally would have been.

"She's pushed herself too much this week. Insisting on working when she still wasn't feeling good. My best guess, she sat down for only a minute on her bed and fell asleep.

"How long was I up there?"

"About half an hour, love." I looked at Rob, confused. He just winked at me, like he was telling me to roll with it.

"Alright. Get some rest. Call me tomorrow, please?" Now my dad sounded worried. I hugged him tight, afraid to let him go.

I was sure Jason at least warned him that he was leaving. He probably wasn't all that happy about it either.

"I love you, daddy." I whispered.

He kissed my cheek as he released me. "Love you too, buttercup. Things will get better, I promise."

My eyebrows creased in confusion, but Rob pulled me out of the house and back into the car before I could give it much thought.

While Rob warmed up leftovers from the night before, I went straight to the bedroom, stripping as I went. Then climbed under my covers. A little later, I heard a soup bowl being set down on the bed side table. Followed by the sounds of someone taking their clothes off.

Rob crawled under the blanket, pulling me into his chest.

"He's leaving me. Why? Why do men keep leaving me? See, if there was anything special about me, people would stop leaving me."

"It's us, it's not you."

I snorted. "That old line, huh?"

"I left because I was scared about the strength of my feelings for you."

"Cop out." I fake coughed.

"Maybe. But it's true. I wasn't ready to be a father. I wasn't ready to be married. And it all came hitting me, fast and hard. So, I ran. It was stupid, and it hurt you. And I will spend the rest of my life proving to you how sorry I am, if you'll let me."

I rolled over and faced him, completely aware that he was wearing only his boxers, and I was only wearing my regular tank top. We'd been sleeping like that all week though. So, it was nothing new.

"Knowing that I was left again, and not because he chickened out, you still want me?"

Rob moved a lock of hair behind my ear. "I told you. I love you. I will always want you. Just ask your cousins. Ask my sister. All this time apart, and I still bugged them for information on you."

"Why did you stop visiting?"

"Because I was afraid I was hurting you. I wasn't ready for that commitment. To be such an adult. For that responsibility. I felt like I was holding you back. I thought if I cut the cord, then we both could finally move on. I can't do that anymore. If you want me, then I am here. Just say the word."

"You will really claim my baby, and be with me?"

He leaned down and kissed me softly. "Yes. I would consider it a privilege to call this baby mine."

I parted my lips just enough to invite him in. I wanted to feel loved. To feel wanted. To feel something besides this darkness in my chest. Very slowly, he accepted the invitation.

I rolled to my back, and he followed. My legs parted, inviting him somewhere else. He growled and pressed against me. Yep, that was the feeling I needed. I reached down, pushing his boxers down. His hands grasped me tight. I had to let go as my back arched.

"We shouldn't be doing this." Rob pulled away.

I used that little bit of space and dipped into his shorts, getting my own handful. "You were saying?"

"Shouldn't." His head dipped down, his lips meeting mine again.

"Should."

His fingers slid back to where they were when I stopped him the other day.

"You don't want this."

"Are you seriously doubting my need right now?" I gave him a pull.

"No, but I'm not the one you want either."

"Yes, you are." My stupid lip quivered.

"No, I am here, and I am willing. But you will hate both of us for it in the morning."

My eyes rolled back as his actions didn't match his words.

"I can help you find a release, but that is all."

"Rob, please."

I started shaking from just the little he was doing. He bent forward kissing me again. Quickly, I wrapped my legs around his waist and pulled him down. I held him right there. He cursed and let go.

He gave me what I wanted. What I needed.

A few minutes later, he stayed hovered over me, much in the same way Jason always did, his body still shaking.

"My memories did not do you justice." He mumbled into my neck.

I laughed. "Yeah? How often did you think of me?"

"All the time. Even during these times. Did you?"

"Most of the time." I frowned as reality seeped back in.

"But not with him." He didn't need to ask. Rob could always read my face.

"No."

"Please tell me you weren't picturing him just now? Lie to me if you have to."

I laughed. "No. I didn't, and I'm not lying."

Rob pulled back and dropped onto the bed next to me, a sigh of relief and thanks on his lips.

"When you hate me later, I will remind you this was all your fault."

"I could never hate you. I do feel guilty for taking advantage of you though."

He kissed my lips sweetly. "You can take advantage of me anytime you want, sweetheart. But I think it would be best if we wait on repeating this until you talk to Jason."

"What? Why? He's leaving. He doesn't want to be with me."

He nodded slowly, his head tilting to the side. "Possibly. It's also possible that he thinks you and I have gotten back together."

"I explained that to him though. I sent him all those messages."

"I know that. But I still think it is best that you talk to him first. Before we make this official."

"Right, like you calling me "love" in front of my dad didn't just do that."

Rob laughed. "I'm just laying the groundwork, sweetheart. And if nothing comes of it," he shrugs, "old habits die hard. Like this." He leaned down and kissed me again, his hand gripped my side and rolled me back to him.

I figured I owed him one, so I didn't fight him. Not even when he lost the battle of wills and rolled me onto my back again. I cackled as he cursed himself a few minutes later.

"Okay, *now* we won't repeat that."

"Ya huh, I heard that before."

Rob jumped off the bed and started pulling clothes back on. "I am going to reheat the soup and stay away from you for a while. I think I just opened a can of worms that wasn't meant to be mine."

I didn't know what that meant, but my body felt more relaxed. Wish I could say the same for my heart. I walked over to my dresser and pulled out an old pajama set. The more I thought about what we just did, the worse I felt. I needed more clothes. The temptation of a man who wanted me, when the other didn't, was too much.

Part of my heart would always belong to Rob since he was my first love. But Jason owned the rest. Given time, I knew Jason would have owned it all.

By the time Rob returned, with the reheated soup, I was bawling again.

"Yep, I was right. Which should help me to keep my hands, and other parts, to myself."

He sounded so sad about that, and it made me cry harder.

He continued staying with me all week, both of us sleeping with more clothes on than the previous week. It killed me that I was basically keeping Rob as a backup plan, it wasn't fair to him. But he wouldn't let me say it anymore. Apparently verbalizing it only made it worse.

Finally, the week ended. I knew Jason wouldn't miss dad's birthday party. I was sure that was why he waited so long to leave.

As per family tradition, we were having another barbecue. And with September nearing its end, the weather was finally beginning to cool. I wore jean pants instead of shorts, and a full t-shirt.

"You ready?" Rob asked, holding the handle to the front door.

"Not in the least."

He chuckled and kissed my forehead. He'd been careful not to kiss me anywhere but there either. And even that had been severely cut back on.

CHAPTER 19

Jason

Hiking was a bad idea. My thigh may do fine on most days, but walking through branches, dirt, rocks, and all sorts of tripping hazards was pushing it. I preferred flat, solid, surfaces. Or hell, sand. I ended up just driving for a while, coming to a stop outside of a bar on the opposite side of town from Marcus' place. I sat in my truck, the one I probably should have remembered I had *before* I bought the plane ticket. Guess I would need to ship it back to Vegas. Or refund my ticket and drive. I didn't really care.

With that last thought. I climbed out and walked inside. It was dark, dirty, and loud. Perfect.

Three beers in, and I felt the edge of my issues start to melt. This was what I needed. Maybe drinking didn't work for Marcus, but he still had a family to hold onto. What was that I decided months ago? I passed my time for a family. I was too old for it.

I had caught a brief glimpse of what it could be like and got my hopes up. It wasn't mine I saw though. It was never meant to be mine. So, I ordered another round. And then another. And another.

I welcomed the advances of the women who came around. It was nice to be wanted. It was nice to not be pushed away for a change.

I woke up as the sun started peeking over the ocean. My head felt like it was going to explode. And my mouth felt like I swallowed a jar of cotton. My stomach felt like Angie gave me her stomach flu.

Angie.

I shot out of bed, looking around. Where the hell was I?

And who the hell was that?

I didn't need them to roll over to know that she was not Angie. The black hair pretty much said it all. I quietly started collecting my clothes and pulling them back on. I kept one eye on the unknown combatant, not sure if they were a friendly or not.

She didn't roll over until I was putting my shoes on. I silently screamed into my fist. Then mouthed a slur of curse words that would make most Marines blush. I held the rest of my things to my chest and got out of there like a bat out of hell. I raced home with only one thought on my mind.

How in the hell did I end up in bed with Rebecca?

I ran inside the house, planning to shower, and scrub at least three times. My memories may be blurry, but I was sure she did some things I hadn't gotten to do with Angie yet.

Yet? Hmph, I would never get those privileges with her. She chose Rob.

I came to a screeching halt when I saw the very unimpressed man standing in the middle of the stairs.

"Uh, hi." I took a step to the side to pass him. He moved with me. So, I stepped to the other side. And he moved again. "No offense, you're a great dancer and all, but I would really like to shower before work."

"Where've you been? Did you get lost while hiking?"

I closed my eyes and cursed. "I'm sorry. I should have called. It didn't take long for me to realize that hiking is no longer something I can do. At least not yet."

He nodded, that dad nod. "Yeah. I had a feeling that would happen. Then what did you do? Because you sure as hell weren't here."

I rubbed my head, feeling gross just thinking about it. "I drove for a bit, then stopped for a drink.

My old Sergeant took the last few steps down, his eyes on mine. "Did you tailspin?"

I must have still been hungover and tired, my eyes watered. "Yes, sir." I retired as a full Major, and I was siring a Captain who was discharged?

"How bad?" At least his voice was softening.

"I don't remember much, but I woke up in Rebecca's bed."

He closed his eyes and cursed. "Do you feel better? Did it balance you out?"

"Not in the slightest. I feel even more off than before."

He put a hand on my shoulder, squeezing it tight. "Then that's not the path you should be on, son."

"Yeah, well, my other path is no longer available."

"Before last night it was. Now, I don't know." He looked sad as he passed by me.

I couldn't resist the temptation to ask, so I followed him to the kitchen. "How was dinner? Is Angie better now?"

He scoffed. "Doubt it. She said she was fine, then basically hightailed it up to her room. Claimed she might have forgotten something. Rob went up and got her half an hour later. Said she had fallen asleep on her bed."

"You don't sound like you believe it."

"Well, her door was closed, yours was open. She was pale as a ghost, and your flight reservation was hanging on your dresser for all to see. You do the math. Rob took her home after. Seems he is staying in her guest room cause his mama is driving him crazy. Good thing she was too nice to leave him alone last night, she didn't look like she was in any shape to drive. Course, I don't know if he is still using the spare room. If you ask me, that boy was just waiting for his opening."

He poured himself a bowl of cereal while he explained all that. I just stared, probably looking like an idiot as he laid it all out.

"Go on, take your shower. We need to leave in 20 minutes."

I fought the urge to salute as I did an about face and marched up the stairs in a daze.

Was he really using her spare room? She hadn't taken him back?

Hope flared in my chest, but then immediately dwindled. If she saw that I was leaving, she would have given up on me. I'd been ignoring her all week. I deleted her messages without reading or listening because I didn't want to be tempted. And now I may have blown everything up.

It wasn't until I was drying off that the full reality of the situation dawned on me. I slept with Rebecca last night. Even if Angie hadn't chosen Rob yet, she sure would now.

Demolition hadn't been my specialty in the military, but it looked like I had finally gotten the hang of it as a civilian.

I needed to know how bad it was. But my pride wouldn't let me call her. So, I aimed my questions at Kyle. I didn't see him at all on Monday, but I did Tuesday. And he didn't wait for me to ask any questions, or for me to even finish getting out of my truck. Just one look at his face told me he was ticked.

"I don't know what the hell you did, nor do I want to. But Rob sure seemed a lot happier when I talked to him yesterday. If you wanted her to pick him, then good job."

I yanked my tool bag out of the cargo hold I put in a couple weeks ago. "What did he say?"

"Nothing really. Angie's been sick but getting better. He's staying with her, trying to make up for leaving. I have a feeling none of us knew the real story behind him leaving. Just the two of them. He seems pretty confident that he's got his girl back. He said there was some other stuff he couldn't tell me yet either. Something about a trip to Vegas a couple months ago."

That got my attention. And had Kyle backing up.

Did she tell him? Why? Why would she tell him?

Unless she told him I was the reason she was keeping him at a distance. If they knew I was leaving, then yeah, he would think he was in.

Even Kyle kept some distance between us over the next few days. And thankfully, Rebecca and I were not assigned to the same sites. When I got my head on straight again, I'd have to thank Marcus for that. Last thing I needed was her hints while at work.

Saturday morning, I helped Marcus set up the table and chairs in the back. He pulled a few other tables out as well since he was expecting more people this time.

A little before one, people started showing up. Around one thirty, Angie and Rob walked onto the patio. She greeted her dad with a big hug, and then some of the others. Her eyes met mine just long enough for me to see the pain. The darkness I was causing. The eyes that reminded me of the calm sands of the desert now looked like the darkness that rolled in before the sandstorm.

I watched her mingle with family and friends for the first hour. I insisted that I run the grill full time today, since it was Marcus' birthday. He relented when Kathy backed me up.

Rob never seemed to stray far from Angie. The only time he left was if she needed something.

"Grubs on." I called out.

A few of the men came over and started loading up trays and platters to carry to the table. Rob too. He came over to grab some of the meat.

"Look, as much as I want to say, get on your plane, and go. I can't. I did that. And now I am paying the consequences. Learn from my mistakes. But if you don't, I want you to know, I'm ready and waiting to catch her." He walked off, leaving me confused about what the hell just happened.

I guess that answered my question on whether he knew, but now I had a whole bunch more that needed answering. I followed them all to the table, taking up a seat near Marcus. Who, like always, sat across from Angie. He gave a little speech, thanking everyone for coming, then said we could eat.

She may have refused to look at me, but I wasn't having the same issue. The woman who would eat anything on a burger a few weeks ago, barely touched it. And that was after she took most of it off. Without a word, Rob traded her for his hotdog. She only ate part of it. And she only drank ginger ale.

Was she still sick?

The two of them moved to the small couch on the patio, looking mighty cozy. Everyone else drank, laughed, drank some more, and played a round of ball together. Angie laughed from the side, her smile not quite reaching her eyes.

"He always did dote on her." Lauren walked up to my side, her eyes in the same direction as me. "She doesn't look much better though, does she?"

"That's what I've been trying to figure out. Marcus and I used to tease her for how much she ate, but not tonight. I didn't want to worry Marcus, so I figured I would keep an eye on her."

Lauren looked over at him, laughing. He was drunk and having fun with his brother-in-law. "Good call. He's a worrywart. Always has been. But you don't need to worry yourself too much. That girl has always had my boy wrapped around her little fingers. It drove me batty when they were teenagers, thinking they were too young. Then he took off. I felt like I lost part of my son that day. Looking at them now, I can see it coming back. I hate that she's sick, but at least it's opening both their eyes again."

I cleared my throat, forcing my eyes to move away. "Guess I won't worry so much then."

She laughed and patted my arm. "We always worry about those we care about. I know you haven't known her for long, but you care about your friend, so you care about her. It's natural. She's not my daughter, but her well-being affects my son."

I nodded and made an effort to change the subject, focusing on those playing ball. Including Marcus, who wasn't running in a straight line. I couldn't tell if that was on purpose or not. He was happy though, and that was what mattered for the night.

As the sun began to fade, people began to leave. Soon it was just the four of us. Angie and Rob moved inside, while I collected trash outside. Marcus was… sort of helping. He kept trying to make a basket with the trash and kept missing.

I collected a pile of serving bowls and pans and carried them into the kitchen. I was wary of what I would be walking into, but they were just silently talking.

Rob looked up at me, standing in the doorway. "I'll wait in the car."

"Rob." She pleaded for something. I didn't know what. He kissed her forehead in a way that made it look like he was saying goodbye.

As soon as he was out of the room, I walked over to the sink. I opened my mouth to say something, but Marcus beat me to it.

"Goodnight, buttercup. I'm glad you're feeling better." He gave her a big hug and a kiss on the cheek.

"Night, daddy." Her voice was shaky, but he was too drunk to notice.

"Oh, Jace. What time does your flight leave tomorrow? We can drop your truck off at the shipping…place and then I can take you to the airport."

I had no idea how his brain was functioning, his feet sure weren't.

"I need to leave by ten to do all of that."

He gave me a very drunk salute then swayed over to the stairs.

Angie hiccupped. "So, you are leaving? Were you even going to tell me? Were you going to say goodbye at least?"

I wiped my sweaty palms on my pants, "I didn't think you wanted me to. You've been pretty cozy with your new little boyfriend. Or is it old boyfriend?"

"That's not fair."

I hmphed and turned to the sink to start washing. "You can go. I'm sure he's antsy to get you home. I'll make sure this all gets cleaned up."

"So, that's it. After everything, that's it? You are leaving me. Not a word, not a "it was fun." Just leaving me."

I spun back around. "You chose him! What was I supposed to do, sit around here and watch?"

"I chose you, you moron!" She stomped out of the kitchen and grabbed her purse. I ran after her.

"Angie, he's been living with you for over a week. He's been taking care of you while you were sick. You have a history together. He's not torn and broken like I am."

"Yeah, and he chickened out just like you are. At least he is man enough to realize it. With him, it was just a scare, with you it isn't. Somebody had to hold my hair every time I puked. Somebody had to be there while I melted after taking the test." Her breath caught. "Someone had to be there when you weren't answering me, when I needed you the most."

She opened the door and tried to leave, but I grabbed her hand. "What are you saying, Angie?"

With her back to me, her head barely turned, she killed me. "I'm saying I'm pregnant. I was hoping to tell you last Sunday, but you weren't here. Instead, I saw your flight information. Even if you stayed now, it would only be for the baby. Not for me. I held out all this time because I loved you. But I won't be with a man who only wants me because of his child. I deserve more than that."

My fingers slackened and I stumbled back, feeling the blow of every one of those words as though they were live grenades being thrown at me.

I blinked and she was gone.

"What the hell just happened?" Surely I heard all of that wrong. None of it made sense.

I jumped when a heavy hand hit my back roughly.

"Easy, you knocked up my daughter and then put your foot in your mouth." Her dad slapped me again and squeezed. "Good luck with that mess. Her mother hit crazy hormones early, too."

He walked back to the kitchen, I turned and followed like a lost puppy.

"Yeah, still not sure what just happened. And I thought you went to bed to pass out?"

He waved a hand. "Psh, nah, I just needed an excuse she would believe so she would feel comfortable enough to speak freely. Take a seat, son, before you put a hole in my floor the size of your butt."

I did as he said, dropping into the nearest chair. "Are you going to kill me now?"

He barked out a deep laugh, not one bit of him looking or sounding drunk in the slightest. He turned the water on and started washing the dishes I had left behind.

"No. If I was going to, it would have been your first night here. I may be a deep sleeper, but it takes a while to get there, to shut all the senses down. I heard her screech when you pulled her into your room. I was running out here to see what was wrong when I saw your door close. I let it go."

"Seriously? Why?"

"Because." He chuckled. "You should have seen the look on both your faces when she walked out that night. At first, I was lost on why you both looked like deer in headlights. Then you made that comment about not recognizing her all grown up. You both had already mentioned making a friend at the airport. I started putting two and two together. Your little stunt that night was the clencher. Then there was the way you two always look at each other, or the way you serve each other's plates at dinner. Little stuff like that. Things you probably didn't even realize you were doing."

I opened and closed my mouth a few times. Completely lost. "Why didn't you say anything?"

He shrugged. "Figured our past was already a big enough obstacle between the two of you, I didn't need to add to it. It's important to learn to work out your problems together." He sighed sadly. "I should have stepped in sooner. What was the issue anyway? I know it wasn't the age thing."

I rubbed my face roughly, trying to force my brain to work. I ended up having to stand up and start moving around again.

"It was a lot of little things. But mainly, she worried she would mess up our friendship." I waved a hand between him and I. "She said you sacrificed enough to give her a stable home after Marta died, she didn't want you doing it again. She was under the belief that you've been happier with me here, a connection back to the life you left for her."

Marcus turned off the water and held onto the counter as he laughed. It wasn't joyful, it sounded almost self-deprecating. I waited him out. Eventually he turned around to face me.

"Am I happy to have someone here who understands? Yes. But that wasn't what made me happy. I like you, Jace. You know I do. You've been a good friend. Mostly, I know what kind of man you are. And I could see how much you cared for my girl. That is what made me happy."

"What about Rob?"

"Rob was a chicken. Unlike Lauren and the rest of them, I know what happened. *I* was the one that held her together when he left." His animosity toward the boy was showing again.

"What happened?"

He dried his hands on the towel then threw it on the table. "When she was 17, they had a pregnancy scare. Up to that point, it was pretty well established that they were going to get married one day. They had college plans and everything. Rob was 18 and getting ready to start classes. Within a few days, he up and left. Personally, I think the idea of a baby made it too real too soon. They were too young. As is, they weren't planning on getting married until after college."

"That's what she meant by him chickening out and his being just a scare."

"Yep." Marcus stepped away from the counter, coming closer to me. "And dollars to donuts, that boy is planning on staying by her side and claiming this kid. He wants to prove he's grown up, that he's changed, serendipity has given him that chance. So now, tell me, Major. Do you love me daughter?"

"Very much so."

"Is she your balance?"

"Being with her gives me more peace than I have felt in years."

"Then get over there and tell her that!" He ordered me, pointing toward the front door.

I groaned and pulled my hair with both hands. "She will think I am only there because of the baby."

"Well, are you?"

"Hell no!"

"Then get your khaki covered butt in that truck and go tell her that!" When I didn't move, he added, in a yell I was all too familiar with, "That was an order, Marine!"

Shoot. It didn't matter how long it had been since he was my commanding officer, my body reacted without second thought. I was out that door, with more than a ghost of a laugh following me.

CHAPTER 20

Angie

I ran out of the house, tears blurring my vision, and jumped in Rob's car.

"Drive."

He started and bolted out of there. "Do you want to talk about it?"

I shook my head as the sobs bubbled out of me again. He touched my head, and I curled up next to him with my head on his lap. Rob rubbed my arm and my back. Which made me remember the massage and I cried harder.

Jason had worked a lot harder than I had that day, and yet he took care of me without my even asking.

How did everything turn upside down so quickly?

I should have given him more of a chance to explain. But the moment he started saying I chose Rob, I had to get out of there. I didn't choose Rob. I told him that in the messages.

Which he obviously never read.

"Hey, we're home." Rob told me softly.

I sat up and walked into my little house. The one that Jason worked through the night to finish. His mark was on it now. I would never be able to *not* see him standing there in the early morning light, finishing a wall he had to have spent half the night working on.

I sank onto the couch and just let Rob hold me.

"Did he say he didn't want anything to do with you or the baby?"

I shook my head.

"So, he does?"

I shook my head again.

"What did he say, Ang?"

"That he thought I chose you. And that you weren't broken like him."

"Oh-kay. And what about the baby?"

I shrugged. "I left while he was shocked. He didn't want me before the baby, why would he now? I deserve someone to be here for me too."

Rob sighed and rubbed my arm again, as he held me to his side. Rob was good to me. He rarely left my side all day. He gave me his food when my own made me sick. He wanted me, he even wanted my baby. He wanted both of us. What more could a girl ask for?

I turned and looked at him. He lifted that ridiculous eyebrow that only men seemed to be able to lift.

"What?"

I climbed onto his lap and straddled him, practically attacking his mouth. He sat in shock for about one second, then joined in. I lost my shirt quickly, his following after.

About the time I started undoing the button on his jeans, he grabbed my hands and held them tight.

"Not right now, sweetheart."

"What? Why? I thought you said you wanted to be with me. You said we were going to wait until I talked to Jason. Well, I've talked to him."

"Yes, but you didn't exactly give him a chance to talk back."

"Not about the baby, no. But his actions in leaving and icing me out for the last two weeks spoke plenty about where I stand on his priorities radar." I leaned in and started kissing him again.

Rob's hands loosened as I pushed against his will power. With a growl, he threw me on my back on the couch. I reached and barely grazed him when he jumped off me and walked away.

"What the hell, Rob?"

"Angie. I love you more than I could ever tell you. But you don't love me. I know, given the chance, you would love me again. But right now, you are in love with someone else. I caved to what I wanted the other day, to what you thought you wanted. But I can't do that right now."

I picked my shirt up off the floor and pulled it back on. The tears started falling again. "I'm sorry. I'm all kinds of messed up and taking you down the pit with me."

His growl sounded more like a whimper, as he zipped his pants back up and sat down in front of me.

"Sweetheart, you have no idea how badly I want to follow you down into that pit. I know I have the power to pull you up, but you aren't ready for me to do that yet. We both deserve to have you heal before we go down that road together."

I laid my head on his shoulder and cried again. And, again, he held me. This time, he kept most of his body away from me. In time, he lowered me to lay on the couch, and he sat on the floor next to me. I was almost asleep when I heard a diesel truck pull in, a knock following soon after.

Rob kissed my head again and whispered, "It was worth a shot." He slid his shirt over his head as he walked to the door.

"Yeah, kind of figured it was you." I heard the sound of keys and a bag getting picked up. "She's on the couch. Good luck."

A moment later, the door closed and someone else was kneeling in front of me. I kept my eyes closed, but I felt the calloused fingers as they combed through my hair.

"Hey." A stupid tear dropped out of my eye. "Come on, sweetheart. Look at me, please."

I opened my eyes slowly, blinking the wetness away. "Why are you here?"

"Because I didn't get to finish back there. There was a lot that I didn't say. That I never have, and I should have. A long time ago."

"Like what?"

"Mostly? That I love you."

I groaned and tried to roll over, not wanting to look at him. He wouldn't let me though, I only got as far as my back. I threw my arm over my eyes, hoping that would help.

"You're just saying that because of the baby. You were ready to leave before you knew."

"I was never *ready* to leave, Angie. I thought I was doing what was best for you. I love you. I wanted you to be happy. If that wasn't with me, then so be it. But I couldn't sit here and watch it. Or let you see how miserable that made me."

I lifted my arm enough to peek at him. He took that as encouragement and continued.

"I shouldn't have jumped to conclusions, but in my defense, the evidence was stacking up against me."

"What evidence?"

"First there was Kyle, warning me that Rob was going to try and win you back. He was planning on trying to get you to remember how good you were together. Then you told your dad that Rob was taking care of you. Finally… you told me not to come over." His voice was shaky, and I hated it.

I rolled back to face him and practically landed on him, throwing my arms around him. He wrapped his arm around me as he buried his face in my neck.

"I explained it all in my texts! Didn't you read them?"

"No. I was so hurt that you didn't want me here. I silenced my phone and hid it on the floor. The next morning, I started deleting them all without reading them. You were right earlier. I was a chicken. I thought you were saying goodbye again. I didn't want to hear it anymore. I'm so sorry. I went into a dark place after that. Darker than I ever thought I would go. I'm not proud of anything I did these last few weeks."

"Me too. When I thought you were leaving me, it hurt so bad. I reacted, and it wasn't in a good way."

He huffed and released me. I sat up, letting him join me on the couch. His arm encircled my shoulders, keeping me tucked into his side. "I probably did worse. I don't want to tell you, but I also don't want you to find out from someone else."

"Unless you slept with someone else, you can't top mine." I mumbled.

Jason's grip on my shoulder tightened. "You slept with him?"

I gulped. "I was in pain, Jason. I thought you left. I needed to feel something besides the pain. It only happened one night. He's kept his distance since then, until we knew for sure what you wanted."

Some very ugly rainbow-colored words came out of his mouth. "I'll take the blame for that one too. If I hadn't been ignoring you, none of this would have happened."

"We both kept too much hidden under the vest. We are both to blame. Let's get it all out in the open now. No more secrets, no more hiding things."

He took a deep breath then blew it out. "I got really drunk on Sunday. More than I ever have before. I still don't remember how it all happened, and I don't want to ask."

It was my turn to stiffen up this time.

"I slept with Rebecca."

"On Sunday? You weren't at dinner because you were drunk and with Rebecca, of all people?"

"Yeah." He sounded like he was worried I was going to knee him in the groin. I wasn't even tempted.

Nope. Instead of yelling or crying, I started laughing. Which I think scared him more. I climbed on his lap and put both my hands on his face.

"I think it's time we say this, so none of this ever happens again."

"What?"

"I love you, Major Jason Smith. Only you. You are the only man I want to be with. Just you and me…and our unborn baby. I don't care who knows it. They will learn to deal. Dad will just have to learn to share. There is no reason why you two can't still be friends."

Jason chuckled and kissed me quickly. "I love you, too Angela Carson. Only you. There will never be another woman for me. I'm pretty sure I've loved you since the moment you knew what a combat engineer was, and you didn't question my leaving the service at such an odd time."

I giggled. "I'm pretty sure I've loved you since you stabbed me with my Epi pen."

He laughed. "I loved you before you told me you were pregnant, and now I love you even more. I thought my time for love and family had passed. And then you walked into my life, or rather, banged your head against it."

I kissed him again, drawing it out this time. It wasn't long before he carried me to the bedroom and placed me on the bed. We didn't speak for quite a while, at least not the kind that counted as a conversation anyway.

We snuggled in the bed, one of his arms under my head, the other one over our baby.

"I guess we need to figure out how to tell dad he doesn't have to take you to the airport tomorrow."

Jason cleared his throat awkwardly, the way he always did when he was uncomfortable or nervous. "About that. He, uh, was only faking being drunk so you would think it was safe to talk. He was eavesdropping from the stairs the whole time."

"He what?!" I grabbed a pillow and buried myself. Jason promptly took it off. "You didn't accidentally kill him when he went for his shotgun, did you?"

"No." Jason chuckled. "He was the one who pretty much had to explain everything to me like a child, then booted my butt out of the house. I didn't think you would let me in, let alone listen to me."

"He did?" That was so sweet.

"Yes. And it seems your father has known about us since day one."

I listened in shock as Jason explained everything that happened after I left, and everything my father said.

"So, we're good? He's good?"

"We're all *very* good." Jason dropped his voice, his hand moving away from my stomach again. I giggled happily.

CHAPTER 21

Jason

Angie and I hid in her little house all weekend. I did remember to send Marcus a message to let him know that all was well. I took a page out of his book and sent him an emoji. Just a basic thumbs up. He sent back one of those GIFs with someone raising their hands in a hallelujah. He then had a pizza delivered to her house. We took that as a sign the family dinner was canceled for this weekend.

We talked about every little thing, making sure there was no room for any more misunderstandings. She even told me about Rob's plan if I bailed on her. Which made Kyle's comment about Vegas make more sense. I had to give Rob credit. It was pretty cool of him to step up like that, even if he was vying for my place at her side. Maybe he had finally grown up.

Ben messaged her at one point, saying he was in town and wanted to hang out. I responded that she was busy and would be for the next fifty years or so. He sent back a simple message.

Ben: I knew it. Good luck… you might want to invest in a cup.

Angie and I both laughed.

We had a long farewell at her car before she went to work on Monday morning. I ran by her dad's place to change clothes, before I headed in. Thankfully, he had already left for work.

I pulled up to the site where Kyle was waiting for me, a grin on his face.

"What are you so happy about this morning?"

He chuckled. "The same reason as you most likely. Well, not exactly the same reason, but close enough."

I shoved his head to the side playfully. "Spit it out already, you're talking nonsense."

"Rob showed up at my apartment Saturday night. I gave him a beer and he spewed it all out. Even his own guilt for leaving her after high school. Congrats on the kid, by the way."

I shook my head and set up the ladder. "Thanks. Just don't go blabbing to everyone. Angie wants to tell them all together. She is already considering Halloween costumes that will do it for us."

"Out of all the things I would rat her out for, I would not take this one. This one is special."

"That she is."

Kyle burst out laughing and started handing me the supplies we needed to do the roof on someone's extended patio edition.

We finished by lunch and were done for the day. I was just about to leave when Kyle called out.

"Hey! Has she told her little group of friends from college yet? They coming out?"

"Um, no. She is calling them tonight I believe. Why?"

"Nothing. Just curious."

"Ya huh." Odd, but whatever.

I went back to Marcus' and packed up my things. I stopped in the kitchen to leave him a note, and instead found a black velvet box with a note under it.

Take care of my girl, Major.

Well, I guess that saved me from making one of the trips I had planned today. I replaced his note with one of my own. In the same spot, I left my receipt from the flight, with a big red X over it. And a small note.

You're relieved of duty, Captain.
I'll take the next watch. Enjoy retirement.

Laughing, I threw all my gear in the back of my truck and drove back to *our* little bungalow. Mine and my girl's home.

After cleaning up, I ran to the store, grabbing supplies for how I wanted to surprise her tonight. My last stop was picking up dinner at the little Cuban place she loved, the one down the street. I kept it in the oven, so it wouldn't be too cold by the time she got home.

As soon as she walked in, she dropped her bags, and jumped on me, wrapping her legs around my waist.

"Hey."

I chuckled. "Hey. How was your day?"

"Fine. The nausea seems to be settling around the same time in the afternoon. I spoke to the teacher next door to me, and she agreed to watch my class when I have to run. The best part though was seeing your truck in the driveway when I got home."

I pulled my head back before she could land the kiss and started walking toward the nearest wall.

"Really? I didn't know you had a thing for trucks." I pinched her butt and she cackled.

It stopped the second her back hit the wall. We stayed there until I finished welcoming her home properly. I didn't put her down until her legs couldn't stay around me anymore. And then I carried her to the kitchen counter.

"Did you make sure that door was locked? We don't need your cousin walking in again. Pretty sure he won't miss anything with you naked like this."

Her face flushed but she was laughing. "I can't believe he saw that and didn't say anything."

I shrugged. "Are you hungry? I picked up dinner earlier."

"Hmm, yes, please."

We did end up putting some clothes on, as she started getting chilly. Then she dove into her Ropa Vieja. After dinner, we sat on the couch and watched a movie. I purposely picked the same one we watched in the airport a few months ago.

I left her there to go prepare my next surprise. She laughed when I set the banana split down in front of her.

"You almost recreated our first date perfectly."

"Our first date, huh?"

"Yep. That was our first date. A blind date at that."

"Really, and who set us up on it?"

"Easy. Hurricane Edith."

I laughed as I sat down next to her on the couch again.

"I hadn't thought of it as our first date when I decided to do this, but I guess that makes this work even better. I would have gotten me a bacon burger, and you chicken strips and fries, but the burger made you sick at your dad's party the other night. I didn't want to risk you getting sick tonight."

She looked at me in shock.

"My eyes have always been on you, sweetheart. No matter where we were in our relationship. Anyway, I figured the Cuban food was a safe bet. And didn't think we needed to revisit the whole cherry thing again either."

She grimaced and shook her head.

"That day was the first day I met you. The day when I realized there was more to my future than I planned, then I ever thought possible." I pushed the spoon through a specific spot in the ice cream and lifted it to her.

She looked down and then up again at my eyes, she was slightly confused, as she pulled the simple band with a simple diamond out of the dessert. Simplistic beauty, just like her. Perfection without the embellishments. I set the spoon back down, as I slid to one knee in front of her, giving her a second to process what I was about to ask.

"Today, I am building on what we started in that airport. We got delayed for a while, but now we are back on course. I want to make what we found together permanent. I want to make sure we have clear skies ahead. You becoming the cherry on top of my life is the best thing I could ever ask for. I love you, Angie. Be my wife? Be by my side forever?"

"Yes. Holy smokes, yes! I love you so much!" She waved her hand in front of her face, like it would actually stop the tears she had coming down.

I slid the ring on her finger and kissed my fiancé. "It's so beautiful, Jason." She sniffled, her eyes still on it. "It looks just like the one mom used to wear."

I moved to sit next to her again and wrapped my arm around her. "That's because it was hers. At least I think so. Your dad gave it to me."

"Really?" I nodded and chuckled at her little squeal. Then laughed harder as she jumped on my lap.

That time I took her to the bedroom, and then ran to put the ice cream away before it melted. I would always obey her commands. I did take the fudge sauce back with me though. I wasn't done recreating and building on what we started in that airport. Except it wouldn't be her lips I was cleaning chocolate off this time. Well, not *just* her lips.

I sat beside her a little later, as she video called her three friends. Showing off me, the ring, and her nonexistent baby bump.

The next morning, Marcus showed up with donuts, tired of waiting for us to come to him. I did finally get to ask him why he forced me to go out with Rebecca that first time. He shrugged and said he was trying to push us out in the open. It just backfired on him. Big time.

After a long morning of debating, and everyone needing to leave for work, we finally caved and let him call everyone to tell them about the engagement, that was the only way he would let us hold back on the baby news.

Angie's mother's side contacted her not much later. They were confused, as Ben never set anyone straight. Which would be why Angie hadn't heard from him in a few weeks, before that recent message. She happily took care of it for him. She told them *everything*. She hoped it would force him to man up and come clean with his family.

At her first checkup, the doctor did one of those picture things, the ones that allowed us to see the baby. Only, she stuck it inside my girl. Since it was hard to tell when she actually missed her period, they were going to have to go based on the baby's measurements. We decided the night I replaced her wall was the night she got pregnant.

Angie still claimed it was the best massage ever.

EPILOGUE

Kyle

"Dude. Will you please take a chill pill and calm the freak down." Rob snapped at me.

I could have snapped back, but the man was going through some serious crap right now. I was working extra hard to be patient with him. He was handling everything with Angie and Jace okay, up until Uncle Marcus called to tell us the news. That was the first time I ever saw the man cry.

"Pacing is me trying to calm down. I can't sit still."

Rob sighed and sat up from his spot on the couch, where he had been for the last week (outside of work), since he showed up looking like death at my door. Right after he left the girl he never got over with another man.

"What's going on? Talk to me. Maybe that will help."

I stopped, about halfway through my return trip to the small counter dividing my kitchen from my living room. I studied him for a minute, then shook my head and started pacing again.

"No, it's fine. You have enough on your plate as it is."

Rob groaned this time, as he pushed himself to stand. He walked around the couch and planted himself in my path. "Talk to me, Kyle. It might help me to focus on something else."

I huffed and walked around him. "Doubt it. Pretty sure this will just make it worse."

His eyes widened in alarm, and he grabbed my arm. "Ang is okay, right? Her and the baby are fine?"

I took a deep breath and patted his shoulder. "Angie and the baby are just fine. Healthy as can be."

Uncle Marcus and I were still the only ones in the family to know that my favorite cousin was pregnant. I felt bad that I was the only one Rob could talk to about all of this, but he was trying to respect Angie's wishes. What made it worse was the fact that I was on Team Jace. I may never have told Rob that, but I was pretty sure he knew.

I loved Rob like another brother, always have. But he screwed up by leaving. He came back a few times, keeping my favorite cousin on the hook. But then, he stopped, and she had to move on. She had to learn who she was without him. And now that he finally pulled his head out of his rear, she had found someone more worthy of her. If Rob had never left, I was sure they would have been happy together for the rest of their lives.

And probably still ratting me out and using me to cover for them.

Yeah… I knew what she was doing. My dramatics made her happy, and I would do anything to keep her that way. Angie had been little more than a shell when they moved back home after her mom died. I was more than happy that my best friend could help put a smile on her face.

There were many times I could have ratted her out. Especially when I would drive her to his work to see him on his lunch break. I came back early one time and wandered around. I saw them coming out of the dressing room, her face flushed, and clothes still twisted. It wasn't until I walked into her house a few months ago, spotting her and Jace in the kitchen, that I started wondering why I always had such rotten timing.

If Rob had never left, they would have been happy. But they both changed while he was gone. They became different people. Jace was the one to finally put her back together again. I loved the man too. He was a good man. He was becoming a good friend.

Rob visibly relaxed. "Then what's wrong? Why are you so worked up?"

I closed my eyes and pinched my nose. "Jace told me today that Angie's little circle is coming down in a few weeks to plan the baby shower."

I saw the struggle in his eyes to focus on my confusing pain, not his. "Why would that bother you?"

I scratched the back of my head awkwardly. "Because that means Nat will be here soon."

He tilted his head. "Nat?" I saw when he realized who I was talking about. His whole face changed. "Oh. Oh. Nat, as in… *Nat*."

"Yeah." I croaked, then cleared my throat.

"When was the last time you saw her?"

"The night before she went home, after finishing her internship with Uncle Marcus… 9 years ago."

"And…"

I sighed and leaned against the couch. "And I promised her I would follow her to Georgia."

Rob shook his head and huffed out a small disbelieving laugh. "Which you never did."

"No. I couldn't do it. The day I went to tell Uncle Marcus that I was leaving, Angie was there. She had a big grin on her face, her Escrow papers in hand. She had bought that pit of house. She wanted help fixing it up. Seeing her smiling face, I couldn't leave her. Not after…"

He licked his lips and looked up at the ceiling. "Not after I did." He stalked back around and dropped onto the couch, one arm over his head.

I followed him and sat in a chair diagonal from him. "It's not anything on you, Rob. You know how sensitive she was to people leaving already before you left. Did your leaving make it worse? Yes. But it's part of who she is."

"Ya huh. So, what did you do?"

"I, uh. I told Nat that I didn't want to start over. I asked her to come here instead. She had just landed a position with a really good firm up there. It wasn't easy for her to get it, as she still needed to do a year of practical training before she could take the exam to get her license. If she had stayed here, she could have kept going with the architect that Uncle Marcus uses. But I had said I'd go with her, and the spot here was gone by then. We argued. That was it. That was the last time we talked. When I broke my promise to her."

"So, we both chickened out. No wonder we get along so well. We're both cut from the same cloth."

"I did not *chicken* out. Angie needed me here." Well, so much for not snapping at him.

Rob dropped his arm and sat up, looking me dead in the eye. "You could have told Nat that you needed to stay longer and help Angie with her house. They are best friends. She would have understood that. Same with Angie. She never would have been mad at you for leaving to be with the woman you loved. She would have loved you more for it. You used her as an excuse, and you know it. You chickened out."

I opened my mouth to argue, then closed it again. He was right. I didn't let myself dwell on it at the time, or any time since. But he was right.

He laughed, although there was no amusement or joy behind it. "We both suck at the women thing. But at least I know that I tried. I may have been too late, but I did come back. It's not too late for you either. Nat isn't seeing anyone." I raised an eyebrow at him, he gave me the first real smile I had seen in days from him. Given it was only half a smile, but it was progress. "I spent two blessed weeks living with Angie. She talked a lot about her friends. Nat hasn't been able to commit to anyone either. She has had one failed relationship after another. And your dear cousin blames you for it."

My grin was full on. "Really?"

He shook his head, then sank back into my couch. "Yes. With Nat coming here, I suggest you do everything in your power to convince her that you are worth it this time. Even if it means following her to Georgia to make your point."

"I can't leave. I have work. Angie has the baby coming. The wedding. Hell, I just renewed the lease on my apartment. Ow! What the hell?" I grabbed the pillow that had just smacked me in the face and threw it back at him.

"Stop making excuses. We both know that Nat will be here when the baby comes, *and* she will be at the wedding. You work for your Uncle for crying out loud! It's not like he is going to give you a

bad recommendation when you apply for a job up North. And…
I'll take over your apartment. I practically live here anyway."

I chuckled. "You just don't want to go face your mother and
explain what happened."

"Hell no. She used Angie to get me to move back home in the first
place."

"What?" Now I was truly shocked.

He laughed and shook his head. "Missy and Kent were talking
about Jace in front of mom. Missy insisted that Jace had a thing for
Angie. Kent laughed it off. Mom called me and told me that if I
ever planned on getting my girl back, I needed to high tail it down
here before my window closed. Mix that with my last girlfriend
telling me I wasn't completely in it with her, and I put in for the
transfer the next day. Mom has already been blowing up my phone
since Marcus started making the calls. I've ignored her. You know
how much mom has always loved Angie."

I rubbed a hand down my face. "That explains so much. I saw her
talking to Jace many times when we were all together. She was
always talking about how good you two were together. She must
have been trying to get him to back off." I cursed. "No wonder he
believed Angie picked you."

"Yep."

"What are you going to do?"

He shrugged and stretched back out on my couch. "I don't know.
Hide?"

I laughed. "That won't help either. Your mom knows where I live
and where you work. She's not going to leave you alone. She's
probably worried that you are going to high tail it out of here
again. And if she finds out how depressed you are about all this,
she won't ever leave you alone."

"Why do you think I am ignoring her calls?"

"Why do you think she is calling? Any day now she is going to come banging on my door because she knows you are wallowing."

He whimpered dramatically. "What do I do?"

"Easy, get a new girl. Make your mom think you had already given up on Angie. That none of this is hurting you as much as it is."

His head turned so he could look at me from the other side of the couch. "Do you really think I am in any shape to start serial dating to find a girlfriend to get my mom off my back? Preferably before their wedding, in four months?"

"Alright, so maybe you find some chick and beg her to pretend to be your girl for the next six months?"

"You…" he stopped talking as he started laughing. "You want me to fake a relationship? And for six months?"

"You're right. Six months isn't long enough. Maybe a year. At least until after the baby is born. That way it will look like you are not affected by either event."

He looked at me like I was crazy. I probably was, but we both knew it was his only option. He wasn't in the right headspace for a real relationship.

"Okay, so now we both have a mission. I have Operation "get Nat back." And you have Operation "get a fake girlfriend." Easy peasy lemon squeezy. We got this."

Yeah… we didn't have this.

THE WEIRD WORLD OF TJ LEE

The Cooper Family Chronicles
- Love, Devotion, and Trust...with a side of Brownies (Levi & Callie)
- For Ellie (Emma & Freddie)
- For Emma (Emma & Freddie Cont./Rick & Rachel)
- Forgive & Forget (Tim & Alicia/Zack & Zoey)
- Avenging Angel (Mitch & Charity)

Dark Protectors (frequent crossovers with the Coopers)
- Daughter For Sale
- Heartbeats
- Sins of the Mother

Million Dollar Duet (Crossovers with the Coopers)
- Million Dollar Angel
- Million Dollar Screw Up

Standalone novels (still have crossovers with the others)
- Finding My Sunrise
- 2 Doors Down
- Last Christmas

The Yin & Yang Collection (you guessed it, slight crossover here too)
- Oil & Water (Mia & Theo)
- Scalpels & Staples (Sheila & Jeremiah)

Indecent Exposure Series (Next Generation of Coopers)
- My Brother's Keeper (Coming This Summer)

To Be or Not To Be
- Delayed

The Silver Moon Collection
- Ivory Snow
- Now Until Forever
- Fate vs Choice

The Cursed Ones
- Revolution
- The Birth of a Queen
- The Witch's Curse

Follow me on Facebook (@tjleebooks), Instagram (@tjlee2.0), Goodreads (tjlee), TikTok (@tjleebooks) and bookbub (@tjleebooks) for updates on new releases.

ABOUT THE AUTHOR

TJ is an avid reader. Reading was always an escape for her in her crazy messed up world. She's always had a vivid imagination. It wasn't until she was locked in her house for a year and a half, with only her two young kids, and two dogs to talk to, that she finally started writing. She found an even better escape.

TJ is a High School English teacher and a single mom. She holds a Bachelor's degree in Cultural Anthropology and Master's in Cultural Responsive Education. Her life motto, one she says with her students regularly, is to "fly your weird flag high!" She wants everyone to learn to be true to who they are. Accept yourself the way you are. Love yourself the way you are.

www.ingramcontent.com/pod-product-compliance
Lightning Source LLC
Chambersburg PA
CBHW072117300726

48975CB00003B/845